GARGOYLES:

A TALE OF TWO MIRACLES

....

DARCY PATTISON

Mims House
Little Rock, AR

Mims House
1309 S. Broadway
Little Rock, AR 72202
www.MimsHouse.com

Publisher's Note: This is a work of fiction. Names, characters, places, and incidents are a product of the author's imagination. Locales and public names are sometimes used for atmospheric purposes. Any resemblance to actual people, living or dead, or to businesses, companies, events, institutions, or locales is completely coincidental.

Printed in the United States.
Publisher's Cataloging-in-Publication data

Names: Pattison, Darcy, author.
Title: Gargoyles : a tale of two miracles / by Darcy Pattison.
Description: Little Rock, AR: Mim's House, 2018.
Identifiers: ISBN 978-1-62944-108-5 (Hardcover) | 978-1-62944-107-8 (pbk.) | 978-1-62944-106-1 (ebook) | LCCN 2018902668
Subjects: LCSH Cathedrals--Fiction. | Gargoyles--Fiction. | Fathers and daughters--Fiction. | France--History--To 987--Fiction. | Architects--Fiction. | Stone carving--Fiction. | Magic--Fiction. | Fantasy fiction. | BISAC JUVENILE FICTION / Fantasy & Magic | JUVENILE FICTION / Historical / Europe
Classification: LCC PZ7.P27816 Ga 2018 | DDC [Fic]--dc23

"Every block of stone has a statue inside it and it is the task of the sculptor to discover it."

– MICHELANGELO

ONE

....

When Laurel disappeared, her father and the villagers and the priests of the Cathedral of St. Stephens searched and lit candles in prayer and pleaded with the heavens for news of her, but they never thought to look up.

It began on a brisk spring morning. Laurel groped for Sloth's cold cheek and caressed the polished stone. From her perch atop a twenty-foot ladder, Laurel looked across the rooftops of the Cathedral at the graceful lines and the gargoyles that capped many gutters. Behind the gargoyles, where the sun couldn't reach, there were still patches of icy snow.

Sloth, named for one of the seven deadly sins, sat in a niche above the main entrance.

Below, Father steadied the ladder and fussed, "How's it look?"

Laurel had scampered up the ladder to check the gargoyle, despite the fact that her father usually insisted that she should stay off ladders with her skirt. "It's not safe," he said. "You'll get tangled up."

But she had helped him carry the ladder and then before he could start up, she grasped the rungs and started climbing. He had sighed but said nothing.

"He is too indulgent," Dame Frances, her old nurse, had always said.

And when Laurel asked what that meant, Dame Frances sniffed and said, "He lets you do whatever you want. And that's not any way to raise a proper lady."

Laurel liked the word, indulgent. She liked what it meant.

Beside her, Sloth grimaced in sleep and she mimicked his contorted face. She had always liked this gargoyle, with its grotesque expression. Maybe she liked him because he was wrapped around the smaller gargoyle and it seemed to her that their sleep was peaceful, even tender, the older protecting the younger.

Her hand went to the large gargoyle's broken wing. The wind grew fiercer, picking up bits of old leaves and blowing them around her face, trying to loosen her hair from her hood.

She called to her father, "You're right. It's badly broken."

Master Raymond, the architect of the cathedral and her father, cursed softly. He hated spending construction money on repairs and there could be a lot of repairs after the severe winter.

"Come down," he ordered.

But she didn't want to go down just yet; she was enjoying the view. Below her, the city of Montague lay quiet, sheltered by the cathedral's shadows like chicks protected by a mother hen. A ten-foot wall surrounded the city and inside, stone houses with thatched roofs crammed together in a jumble of streets.

"Laurel. Come now." Father shook the ladder gently.

With a sigh, she balanced by holding onto the gargoyle's leg with one hand and the ladder with the other. She stepped down to the next rung. But the rung gave way with a crack and she flailed, almost falling. Her weight, though, pulled the gargoyle forward and it tumbled, scraping out of its niche and plummeting toward her father. Laurel swayed and screamed and somehow her foot found the next rung, and both hands found the ladder.

Stone crashed onto the cobblestones below.

Someone cried out.

Then, silence.

Twisting around, she saw a splotch of red spread across the ground, surrounded by broken chunks of stone. "Father!"

Laurel scrambled down the ladder, her breath catching a couple times at how shaky it was without Father holding it. At the bottom, she spun around and—

"Ooomph!" Something smacked into Laurel.

Hands grabbed at her, kept her from falling. A voice yelled, "Hey! Watch out!"

She blinked uncertainly at a scrawny boy, a Rover from the look of his tall boots and that wide leather belt.

Abruptly, the boy turned her loose and held up his hands in a gesture of apology.

Laurel looked around wildly. Where was Father?

"I'm here, Laurel. This boy pushed me aside just in time."

"I'm sorry I fell on you, sir."

"No, no," Father said. "You saved me. Thank you."

She wanted to run to her father, to embrace him, to make sure he was all right. But she controlled her panic and merely nodded at him.

Still flustered, she turned her attention to the boy. It was his red cape she had seen spread out on the ground.

Now, the boy's feet were widely planted, braced against the wind, which had grown even fiercer. He wore a wool-knit cap, but curly dark locks escaped and whipped about.

It wasn't an uncommon sight; traveling entertainers often stopped in the town of Montague. The Cathedral of St. Stephen drew many pilgrims and the pilgrims drew those who made money from the pious. But this was the first Rover of the spring.

Laurel swayed in the wind and the boy clutched her cloak again to steady her. "Hey! Don't blow away."

"Turn me loose." Her voice was tight.

He dropped his hands and stepped away, but then stopped to tip his head back and back, staring straight up, perhaps all the way to the top of the cathedral's spires. Because of the cathedral, devotion to the church was common here in Montague. But this was different. Emotions swept across the boy's face: wonder, a straining to see better. Then a peace smoothed his features.

Laurel tilted her head and studied the boy. Her father's face went through a similar change every morning. Father loved his cathedral and not just because he was the architect. He loved it for its beauty, for its soaring towers that pointed toward "our gracious Lord who sits enthroned in the heavens." A Rover boy interested in a cathedral, though, was as out of place as a saint in a rowdy tavern.

On the other side of the town square, someone yelled, "Jassy!"

The boy startled. "Oh, I forgot! Antonio! He needs—" And without finishing, he loped away.

Curious now, Laurel stared at the brightly painted Rover wagon that sat under a bare-limbed linden tree, a gaudy splash of color in the dreary landscape. Two other people—Rovers, she supposed from their bright capes—stood near the wagon, perhaps an older man and a girl.

Laurel sighed. They would do some sort of show later, probably during lunch when the square and market were the busiest. She'd hear all about it later at the tavern.

Turning back to her father, Laurel said, "I'll put up the ladder and clean up this stone."

He held a chunk of the broken statue, a nose. Sighing deeply, he tossed it aside and pulled her into a hug. "Are you hurt?"

"I just climbed down the ladder. You dodged Sloth. Are you hurt?"

"I'm fine. That's just another statue we have to replace,"
he said. "But right now—" He stopped to cover his mouth
and cough, then continued, "—we have an appointment
to talk with Father Goossens in an hour. I'll go back to the
tavern and pick up what I need and meet you at the Father's chamber."

Laurel nodded. She usually attended all the meetings
with the cathedral chapter, the priests and clerics who
oversaw the building of the cathedral. Her mother had
died in childbirth, leaving Father to care for her. Her
nursemaid, Dame Frances, took care of her until she was
three, but since then, she had tagged along everywhere
with Father. Dame Frances had been her Sometimes-
Mother until last year when her husband had moved the
family to Chantelle, some thirty miles away. Now, at fourteen, Father depended on her sharp memory when he met
with the priests.

She went to the work shed, trundled back a wheelbarrow and started throwing broken stone into it. Sometimes
she paused to turn over a broken bit: a crooked finger, a
twisted smile, or a bulging eye. She ran a finger across the
polished stone eyelids and closed her own eyes, trying to
memorize its feel. When something was intact enough to
study, she put it aside to take back to her worktable to try
to copy. Laurel wanted to be a stone carver and already
had a set of small tools. Whenever she had a chance, she
was working at the stone. It had taken her a long time just
to learn to make a smooth, flat surface. She secretly honed

the stone until it pleased her, and when she had finally shown her father the flat stone, he had swelled with pride. He showed it to Master Benoit and the other masons and carvers. After that, she had dozens of teachers, everyone eager to help the architect's odd daughter.

Laurel knew what they said behind her back, that this wasn't a woman's work, that she would give it up soon. But meanwhile, she learned whatever they would teach. After all, she had grown up with the cathedral and the masons; it was the family business. She heaved up the wheelbarrow handles and shoved it toward the rubble pile near the west end of the cathedral. She would dump the broken stone there, to be used later as fill between the cathedral's inner and outer walls.

Maybe Father would let her carve the new Sloth herself. No, she wasn't ready. But soon—soon! —she would be carving statues for the Cathedral of St. Stephens by herself.

TWO

....

H alf an hour later, Laurel heaved on the heavy oak door of St. Stephen's Cathedral and squeezed through the crack before— Clang!—the wind slammed it behind her.

Instantly, it was silent, but welcoming. She threw back her hood, took off her cloak, and then paced beneath a row of arches along the north side of the cathedral. Her father would be waiting, but as usual, Laurel took the time to marvel at the paintings of the twelve apostles in the choir area, six on either side. Streaming in from the stained glass above, colored light played across the apostle's features. She didn't know which she loved best, the stone carver's workshop with its swirl of noise and dust, or the comfort of this odd family of twelve. Doubting Thomas's worried eyes, Judas Iscariot's blazing eyes, and the Big Fisherman, Peter's kind eyes—she had grown up with these men watching over her. She nodded to them, and then turned to curtsy to the painting of Mother Mary and baby Jesus that hung above the door to the priest's hallway. She had never met her own mother, but always pictured her like this, soft and warm.

Laurel opened the door to the priest's hallway and heard her father's voice. The door to the Father's room was open and she entered. Father Goossens was seated behind his desk, drumming his long ink-stained fingers on his ledger. Her father, Master Raymond, was seated across from him, his cloak flung back over the chair.

Master Raymond was saying, "—must start the west tower this year. It is madness to delay."

"No, there's no money," Father Goossens said.

"No money? Pah!"

Laurel edged into a chair at the side of the conversation and listened, trying to watch both men so she could discuss this with her father later. But the argument was familiar. Clerics always complained of a shortage of funds during the winter, but come spring, they found money to build; all the masons said so. Cathedrals took decades to build, already forty-eight years for the Cathedral of St. Stephens. Only the west tower remained, a project of a mere eight-to-ten years.

Now, Father Goossens clasped his arms across his broad stomach. "The Cardinal himself—the Cardinal! — is coming here to offer mass. Think what that means. For our town, for our priests."

"An honor, of course, your Grace," said Master Raymond.

"Much more than that," Father Goossens said. "This year, our money will go toward making his visit something that no one will soon forget."

Laurel studied Father Goossens, trying to understand. Five years ago, he had moved from a southern town to take over at St. Stephen's Cathedral. At first, his *lingua* d'oc, or southern dialect, was a problem, but he quickly learned the local dialect and put his own stamp on the construction. With the east tower finished, though, he could claim his job was done, and, if he wanted, he could move on to bigger cities, bigger cathedrals. And he deserved it, she decided. His leadership had made a difference in the building project, keeping it organized and on track.

But he didn't need to move on; St. Stephens could offer him even more. The new tower, her father's design—it was a work such that would bring glory to the Lord. And what priest would want for more than that? Smiling, she said, "The Cardinal's visit will be good for Montague and the Cathedral."

Master Raymond added, "The east tower will be ready for the Cardinal's visit on mid-summer's eve. A couple of stone carvers can be assigned to finish detail work. We'll be ready."

"Good." Father Goossens looked down at his ledger, "And after the Cardinal's visit, you must follow the stone and find other work."

Father jerked like he'd been slapped. And Laurel could do nothing but stare at the priest. In fact, she realized she was still smiling. Was Father Goossens telling Master Raymond he had to find a new building project?

"But—" Master Raymond tried to speak.

Looking up, the priest stared directly at the architect. "And, of course, we will continue to pay for your room at the tavern. Until midsummer's eve. After that, you're on your own."

"You can't—" He sucked in a breath, and it came out as a hacking cough. Quickly he covered his mouth and coughed again.

Father Goossens leaned away from Master Raymond and crossed himself. "That's a nasty cough. Laurel, have you been giving him herbs for that?"

Numbly, she nodded. Like many other town folk, Father had gotten sick about mid-winter. But his cough was still lingering. She dosed him regularly with herbal teas and with the coming of spring, he should be rid of it for good.

Recovered from his coughing, Father said, "Are you telling me that after ten years, I must move on?"

"Yes. Get the cathedral ready for the Cardinal," Father Goossens said, "You've been a faithful and skilled architect. Finish your job with the same care to details and I will provide you references to other cathedral projects."

Unable to sit still, Laurel jumped up and stepped to the window. Father Goossens's audience chamber was in the east tower of the cathedral; from here, the bulk of the red-stone cathedral was visible. She had watched her father direct the construction of the east tower for her entire life. As the height of the walls grew, Laurel had grown, too. Her childhood was entwined with those red stones: scampering up and down scaffolds, sliding down ramps, listening to masons argue about the quality of a certain stone, or trading chisels, or arguing about every part of the construction. She knew as much about the east tower as her father—but she loved it more.

"Will you just look at this before you decide anything?" Master Raymond picked up a package that leaned against his chair.

Father Goossens sniffed and rolled his eyes. But he waved his hand in permission.

Smiling to herself, Laurel helped her father unwrap the bundle, unwinding long cloth strips to reveal a drawing that captured her anew. Sketched in red ink—imitating the red stone—was the completed cathedral, including the west tower. Master Raymond had taken over as architect when Master Clavel had died ten years before but had to continue Master Clavel's plans for the east tower. In the west towers, Master Raymond finally had the chance to use his own concepts.

The western transept, or arm of the cathedral, would have an octagonal central tower with two fat rounded turrets rising above the central tower. Laurel adjusted the easel they had brought for the drawing and her father set the drawing in place. Laurel moved it a fraction to the right.

Ah, perfect lighting. No, it was heavenly lighting.

She sent up a swift prayer that it would find favor in Father Goossens's eyes. Truly, only a stone heart could resist this drawing.

"Come, look," Master Raymond said.

Father Goossens heaved himself out of his chair. He was clean-shaven and tonsured, or bald on top, like all clerics here. His steps were heavy, measured. Stopping in front of the drawing, he clasped his hands behind his robe and leaned forward to study it, tilting his head first this way, and then that way. His inky fingers hovered just above the surface, tracing the outlines of the west tower. "Magnificent! The best I have seen."

Joy swelled up in Laurel. "Then, you'll—"

"But we won't build this year."

Master Raymond repeated dumbly, "Not build?"

"Have you heard nothing I said?" Father Goossens said. "The Cardinal comes. And the cathedral is officially finished. We will never build this west tower."

"Excuse me, Father?" An altar boy dressed in a frayed tunic stood in the doorway. "The new mason has sent ahead a message. He arrives at noon today."

"Thank you, my son."

"Yes, Father." The boy backed away.

"Master Raymond, we're done," Father Goossens said. "Come back at lunch to meet Master Gimpel."

"The carver of gargoyles?" Master Raymond said. His voice was strained, as if it had been stretched and was about to break.

Laurel had heard of the strange mason and had been looking forward to meeting him. But with Father Goossens's news that her father would be the architect of St.

Stephen's Cathedral for just a few more weeks, everything had changed.

Quietly, Laurel rewrapped the drawing and handed it to her father. He put it under his arm and pulled his cloak over his shoulders. Laurel felt like a dog that had been beaten by its master. Seeing her face, her father patted her shoulder, smiled weakly, and said, "We'll be fine."

But at the door, he turned and tried again. "Surely after the Cardinal's visit—"

Father Goossens was just easing his bulk into his chair, but he looked up and cut off the architect's question. "Master Raymond, the answer is no."

THREE

L aurel pushed out into the square, trying to think of nothing but a warm bowl of soup for lunch. On the other side of the town square, a noisy crowd roared with laughter.

Curious, Laurel saw the crowd was around the Rover wagon.

Seeing her glance, Father said, "Go on. It will take your mind off things. I'll see you at the tavern in a few minutes."

Usually such things didn't interest her, but remembering the boy from that morning, she said, "I won't be long."

Laurel went to stand at the back of the crowd; even on tiptoe, she could see nothing. She was tiny, like a goldfinch among crows, her father always said. She easily squeezed through tight spaces in the throng until she pushed to the front. The colorful wagon formed a backdrop for a peculiar dance: a black bear shambled on hind legs around an old man—Antonio, she guessed. He was stoop-shouldered and balding. The bear's fur was clean and brushed, and he wore a strip of red leather around his neck, a collar. He looked almost civilized. Except the eyes, which were black and wild.

Laurel shivered, and, though the crowd protected her from the wind's blast, she drew her cloak closer. She should have turned away, should have gone home to Father. But the bit of color, the drama—something kept her there, watching.

A black-haired girl crouched beside the wagon, beating a tambourine and chanting. Antonio stamped and twirled in time to her beat, circling the bear. It swiveled its head from side to side to keep an eye on the old Rover, who was surprisingly graceful for an old man.

Now, he speeded up, stamping and twirling closer and closer to the bear. The tambourine paused suddenly, and in the silence, Antonio darted between the bear's outstretched arms, patted its chest, and then skipped lightly away.

Laurel let out her breath. She hadn't even realized she had been holding it as Antonio had inched closer and closer to the beast. A slight smile, an extra flourish of his hand—the old man was enjoying this, Laurel realized. Even more surprising, she was entranced with the spectacle.

"Watch the Dance of Death!" The boy who had saved Father was passing his woolen cap to collect coins. His uncovered head was a shaggy tangle.

Studying the bear, its claws massive and yellow, a shiver ran down Laurel's spine. The raw animal scent came to her now on the wind and she turned slightly to avoid it.

Off to the side where she now gazed, the rover boy had stopped his slow circuit of the crowd and stood silent. She followed his gaze back to the cathedral and its spires, which shot into the evening sky like solid stone prayers.

When she turned back, the boy stood beside Laurel. "I am glad I was there to push your father aside. I was studying the cathedral; it's so majestic."

"The most beautiful cathedral in all the land," she agreed. She didn't say that she found his fascination strange for a Rover.

"Jassy, the cap!" Antonio hissed.

Now she remembered that Antonio had called him Jassy that morning. She rolled the name around in her mouth: Jassy. Somehow, the foreign name suited him. But even while she repeated the name, Antonio edged nearer and nearer to the bear. Now, Laurel was holding her breath again.

Be careful, she wanted to call.

Jassy shook the cap toward Laurel. "Coins to watch! Watch the Dance of Death."

"Why call it that?" She was suddenly angry at this Rover band, taking such chances. She'd seen too many accidents in the building of the cathedral, attended too many burials.

Jassy leaned close and whispered, "The bear is a pet. Don't worry." Then he called louder, "Coins to watch!"

Just as she suspected. Entertainment such as this was always a fraud in some way. Still—she shivered—she was glad it was just a show and not real. And she was enjoying it. She groped under her cloak and found a copper coin in the hidden pocket of her skirt. Her heart beat fast with the sudden thought that maybe soon, she and Father would be begging for coins, too. But she dropped the coin into Jassy's cap, anyway. She would worry about Father's work later.

"Thank you, miss." Jassy bowed with a flourish of his red cape, and then continued around the circle. "Look at the skill of the dancer! See how he escapes the beast's embrace."

At this cue, Antonio spun around right in front of the bear, while the bear raised and lowered his claw several times. It seemed like the bear was spinning the old man like a top. The tambourine picked up the pace, beating in rhythm to the spinning.

"Ohhh!" Laurel became mesmerized like the rest of the crowd, laughing now at this bit of nonsense.

Jassy dodged here and there, catching up coins tossed at Antonio's feet.

Across the circle, a fat housewife staggered, and then was shoved aside by a ragged boy. His nose was bright red from the cold. A dozen or so other boys shouldered aside the on-lookers and joined their leader. They wore filthy tunics and patched trousers. Two or three wore boots, but the others had rags wrapped around their feet. Thieves and pickpockets. Just another way to make money from the pious who visited the Cathedral of St. Stephen. The first boy briskly swung his arms to warm up, then jabbed his cold-chapped hands into his armpits and stamped his feet in time to the Rover's dance.

Without missing a beat, Antonio nodded at Jassy, catching his attention. The old man ran a finger across his neck. *Time to stop?* he seemed to ask.

Jassy jingled the coins in the cap, and then shook his head, no.

At the tinkle of coins, the filthy boy was suddenly alert, like a hound that had caught scent of a prey. Looking at Jassy's cap, he suddenly grinned.

Laurel stiffened and tried to call out. But a blast of wind took her words. And then it was too late for a warning.

The boy picked up a handful of pebbles and lobbed them at the bear.

The bear whirled and growled. Antonio jumped around to the bear's face, caught its attention and crooned to it in Rover language. The crowd laughed, thinking it was just part of the act. Antonio motioned for the girl to continue her beat and chant. She shook her head and jabbered at him, but he waved again, insistent.

Laurel gripped her cloak closer against the wind, choking back fear.

Three other boys scooped up pebbles.

Jassy dashed toward them: "No! You'll make the bear mad!"

He was only one boy, though, against a gang. They flung their pebbles, hitting the bear. It twisted back and forth searching for the source of the aggravation.

Around her, the crowd exploded with laughter at this new twist.

Jassy charged the gang's leader, but they easily knocked him to the ground, Jassy's cap spraying money onto the cobblestones. Before Jassy even looked up, the boy and his friends had scrambled about grabbing coins and they were pounding away.

But while Jassy lay sprawled on the ground, the bear bellowed his anger. It lashed out in all directions, forcing Antonio to duck, collapsing to the ground.

Now the bear dropped to all fours, snarling and baring his teeth. Antonio was back on his feet, but crouching eye-level with the bear, still trying to capture its attention. In one hand, he held a length of rope to tie to the bear's collar to use as a leash. Antonio's hand was creeping toward the bear's face.

If the dance before had entertained the crowd, it was nothing compared to this *pas de deux*. The town square was silent, everyone watching the bear, the man, the bear, the man. The slow hand reaching toward the bear's nose. The lips that rose to bare gleaming teeth. The gentle hand that touched the bear's nose and stroked it. Calming. Crooning. Tying a rope to its collar.

Laurel's heart pounded frighteningly fast. Antonio was almost there. It was almost over.

From across the square came the sound of the boys laughing. "Dumb Rovers."

And suddenly, the beast clamored in rage and a mighty claw slashed out. Antonio danced aside, nimble, graceful; but his feet tangled in the rope so that he hesitated the barest of moments to keep his balance.

Laurel cried out, "No!"

Claws. Slashing at the man's leg.

He screamed, a cry of rage. And on his thigh, Laurel saw bright lines of blood.

FOUR

··

J assy was there instantly, taking the bear's rope from
the old man's hand and pulling the bear gently toward the wagon.

The rover girl shouted at the crowd, "Go!"

And they slunk away.

Meanwhile, Laurel rushed to the old man and knelt. At
the sight of so much blood, she shrugged off her cloak
and wadded it up to press against the slashes.

Jassy was beside her now and raised an eyebrow. "You
know how to tend his wounds?"

She had often tagged along with Dame Frances when
the good Dame was called to tend a mason or quarryman
and had learned herbs and how to treat an injury. Since
Dame Frances had moved last year and the town lacked a
proper doctor, Laurel had been asked to do more and
more nursing.

"Yes," she answered Jassy, "but I need my herbals."

The old man groaned, and his eyes blinked but stayed
shut. Jassy brushed hair from his eyes and murmured,
"Stay still." Then, to Laurel, he said, "I'll keep his bleeding
under control. Hurry."

Laurel dashed the few blocks to the tavern, ran upstairs
to the room she shared with her father, grabbed her

basket and sewing things—without seeing her father anywhere—and ran back to the square.

Between the rover girl and Jassy, they laid the old man inside the Rover wagon.

"I'm Laurel. What's your name?" Laurel asked the girl.

"Ana-Maria."

"Can you boil water for me?"

The two girls worked together, trying to make Antonio comfortable, while Jassy went out to care for the bear.

When the water boiled, Laurel brewed a sleeping potion that they helped the old man drink. It worked quickly, and Laurel soon had Antonio's wounds sewn up and bound.

"You'll need to keep this clean," she warned Ana-Maria.

"Yes. We need a place to camp until he can travel."

Laurel nodded approvingly: Ana-Maria was practical. Laurel said, "There are caves in the foothills just west of here. Good springs for water, too. I'll come find you tomorrow and look at the leg."

Ana-Maria still held the old man's hand, but she nodded. "Let me wash the blood out of your cloak for you. Where should I leave it?"

"At the tavern." Finally, able to look around, Laurel gaped at the blur of color in the Rover cabin—the first time she had been in one. But she was too tired to focus on the musical instruments hanging on the wall or the smell of strange spices. She needed food, a good hot lunch.

Outside, Jassy stopped her as she tried to leave. "For this—what do we owe you?"

She held up a hand. "Nothing, you saved my father."

"Still, something for your skill with herb and needle?"

This time, Laurel answered as Dame Frances had always answered: "Go and give alms, for it is the Lord who heals."

He nodded and said gruffly, "Thank you. Still it is our way—if you need anything, just ask. I would repay this debt and will do what I can to help you in any way."

"Thank you," Laurel said solemnly.

FIVE

....

As hungry as she was, Laurel only had time for a hunk of bread and a quick bowl of broth eaten standing up in the tavern kitchen. Quickly, Laurel straightened her tunic, smoothed back her hair and ran back to the cathedral to meet the new mason. She wondered where her father was. He was probably talking to other clerics, hoping to convince someone they should build this year, so he could keep his position as architect.

At the cathedral, an altar boy sent Laurel up to the sculpture room to meet Father Goossens. She found him seated on a low wooden table, slightly slumped, eyes closed. Probably napping after a big lunch.

But she couldn't sit still, not after the bear dance. Without waking the priest, she started uncovering gargoyles.

Unheated, frigid in the winter, the room was pleasant in the summer with the windows open, a comfortable, well-lit workroom. To protect the sculptures from the winter's bitter cold, she had helped bury them in hay last fall, giving the room the look of a stone stable. Now that spring was in the air, it was time to pull the statues out to work on them again.

She pushed into the hay, pleased to be able to shove something around. At the first mound, she knelt and swept away clumps of musty hay to reveal a gargoyle. Of all the statues, Laurel loved the gargoyles best for their distorted or grotesque features: hunched backs, bloated faces, bulging eyes or claws instead of hands. Most were decorative. But for reasons lost to history, carvers often drilled a hole through the center, and the gargoyles were set at the ends of gutters to spew out rainwater.

When she was only five years old, her father had put a tiny gargoyle—a bird with a long neck and huge, sharp claws—into her hands. "This will protect you always," he said solemnly.

Dame Frances had scolded him. "You'll frighten the child and give her nightmares."

But Laurel had turned it over and over in her hand, learning its curves, its sharp edges, taking comfort in the tiny bit of stone. For days, she carried it in her apron pocket, stroking it and talking to it. The gargoyle still sat on the shelf beside her bed, where it now protected her dreams. As she had grown older, the gargoyle statues stopped being scary and became comical with their exaggerated or deformed limbs and features. Now, only the very ugliest seemed scary to her.

The gargoyle she had just uncovered was so fat that she couldn't reach all the way around its pink marble waist. Standing about two-feet high, it had coarse, bloated features, a villainous low forehead, a huge belly and a lolling tongue.

When he had finished it, Master Benoit had said, "This one is Greed. Remind you of anyone?"

The way the statue folded its arms over the belly—of course, it was Father Goossens. The stonemasons' sense of humor eventually put every priest into a statue or gargoyle.

Suddenly, her anger at the decision to end the cathedral construction spilled over: she shoved the fat figure and it toppled, barely missing her foot. Fortunately, the piles of hay softened the fall and dulled the thud. And now her own emotions scared her, they were so intense. Laurel collapsed onto the hay and heaved with unshed tears. Change was coming and coming fast and the slow burn of anger spilled over. Decisions were being made that would change her life, and no one cared if she agreed or not.

At last, her emotions dribbled away, and Laurel shoved up on one elbow. She was glad to see that Father Goossens still slept.

She stroked Greed's hard polished tongue and poked the rigid belly. As usual the hard stone pleased her: she wanted to learn to shape rock like this. Sculptures weren't just to be gazed upon; they demanded to be touched. In some ways, the cathedral itself was one giant sculpture, and she had examined almost every stone. She knew the feel of the cathedral right down to its smallest statue.

Shaking off her frustration, she looked around and decided to uncover statues and line them up near the door. It would make it easier to rake up the hay later. Laurel stood and bent to wrap Greed in a bear hug. Staggering under his weight, she carried him to the front wall.

"Excuse me, Father." The same altar boy from earlier stood in the doorway. He looked over his shoulder nervously. "Someone to see you, Father." He quickly crossed himself.

Laurel wondered where her own father was. He was supposed to meet them here.

Father Goossens roused himself and coughed. "Um, yes. I was just praying." He heaved himself down from the table, rocking slightly on his feet before regaining his balance. After a mighty yawn, he said to the altar boy, "Send him in."

A man entered, sliding his left foot before him, and then shifting weight quickly to step with the right leg in a rolling limp. Each step was punctuated by a muted clink from a bag of tools that he carried in his right hand. Slide, step, CLINK.

The mason set down his bag, threw back his hood and shook Father Goossens's hand. "Master Bergin Gimpel, at your service." He bowed to the priest and then to her.

Laurel was on his right side, so until he turned toward her, she hadn't noticed his face. Now, she stood transfixed. What kind of man was this? He wore a black patch over his left eye. Laurel wondered why he bothered, because an empty eye socket couldn't be any worse than the rest of his face. The right side of his face was a classic profile: a soft brown eye, long eyelashes and an elegant, arched eyebrow. The left side of his face, though, was twisted and scarred: rough, pebbly skin, missing eyebrow and missing ear. It was like a rough statue that needed to be polished smooth. Laurel didn't think he'd been burned—she had tended a few burns with her herbs—but couldn't imagine what else could have caused his deformity.

"Laurel, this is the gargoyle carver that I met last year at the St. Assisi Monastery. He agreed to come this spring to finish our gutters."

The man grinned, and Laurel realized his mouth was normal on both sides, with full red lips and a smile that tried to disguise the ugly half of his face. "Truly, people do call me the Gargoyle Man, and not just for my sculptures, either." He motioned to his face and laughed. It was a peaceful laugh, though, not a bitter one.

Laurel started to relax.

Master Gimpel set down his bag of tools and bent to examine the Greed gargoyle. His hands fascinated Laurel. They were graceful, with long fingers. His hands were scarred, too, but she wasn't surprised at that because most masons' hands were burned with the quicklime they used to mix mortar. He had obviously been a mason for a long time.

Father Goossens asked, "What do you think of our friend, Greed?"

"Nicely carved, nicely polished."

At that, Laurel decided she liked Master Gimpel. Master Benoit would have been pleased with that curt compliment of his work. The only thing she disliked was Master Gimpel's eye patch. She vowed to always stand on his right side.

She curtsied. "Master Gimpel, welcome to the Cathedral of St. Stephen. My father is Master Raymond, the architect here. I am called Laurel."

"Lady Laurel." He stood and bowed in return. "Has your father said when the rest of the masons will arrive?"

Father Goossens cut in, "Where is your father anyway?"

Laurel shrugged, "He was supposed to meet us here." Worry trickled through her, and she struggled to keep from frowning. He was probably talking to anyone he could about the Cardinal's visit and the construction of the west tower.

The priest turned to Master Gimpel and answered his question, "Our cathedral chapter decided to hire only two other stone carvers this year. We only need to install these statues and gargoyles—" He waved at partially uncovered stones. "—add a few more here and there and finish up details. The Cardinal will be here at midsummer's eve for a festival. Any detail that might be visible to the crowds must be finished by then."

"Ah—pomp and circumstance instead of construction. It happens to every building project at some time or other." Master Gimpel shrugged and then his brow furrowed. "There will be a full summer of work for me, right?"

"Of course. We still need gargoyle gutters on the west wall since there won't be a tower there. That should keep you busy," Father Goossens said.

Looking from Laurel to Father Goossens, the Gargoyle Man asked, "Will you build again next year?"

"No," said Father Goossens. "The cathedral is so large now that it is half empty during mass."

"But, without the west tower, it will look lopsided," said Master Gimpel.

"Exactly," Laurel cried. "The Cathedral of St. Stephens will not be finished until the west tower is built."

Father Goossens brushed the hay from the bottom of his robe and said, "Child, this is not your affair. Take Master Gimpel and find your father and introduce them. I have other duties that call."

Master Gimpel bowed and Father Goossens bowed back.

Laurel sighed in exasperation. Why did he have to call her "Child"? And where was her father? And why didn't Father Goossens listen to Master Gimpel? She flipped her skirt, shaking off the straw. After wading through the hay, she'd have to stop in the tavern courtyard and wash off at the pump before she ate supper.

"And Laurel—"

"Yes, Father."

"Don't forget your confession later. I'll tell the other priests to direct you to me."

She groaned. "Yes, Father."

SIX

....

Laurel hunched cross-legged beside her father on the bottom bed, a blanket draped over her shoulders like a shawl. It had been a long afternoon of talk and gossip with the new mason. They had finally decided on what sculptures Master Gimpel would start on after he set up his work area. Then over supper, gossip about other building projects filled the time until Laurel was too sleepy to continue. Father had come upstairs shortly after.

Now, Laurel yawned, longing for sleep, but she and Father needed to talk.

"Father Goossens liked your design," she said.

A tall candle lit the whitewashed room with a cheery glow. On one wall were their beds, two wide shelves covered with hay mingled with sweet-smelling herbs. Opposite were two narrow shelves for their few belongings. Under these sat a rough-hewn table with one chair and a stool. Her damp cloak was spread out over the table, still drying.

"Was the good Father angry when I didn't come back?"

"No," Laurel said. "There was Master Gimpel and then he was off on other business."

"I heard about the Rover." Father's words were calm, but his eyes flashed. He stood and started to pace. "An old man and a crazy bear. Will he be all right?"

Father was angry. He only asked about the Rover to distract them both, Laurel thought. She stood, too, wanting to comfort him, but he turned away and paced back toward the door. So, she just answered his question, "The old man will be fine as long as the cut doesn't get infected."

Pacing back to the bed, Father stooped and picked up her blanket that had fallen when she stood. He flapped it angrily, and then tossed it onto the bed. When it tumbled off, he wadded it and hurled it at the wall. It fell onto the upper bed.

"Father Goossens may think he can stop this, but he can't. My designs—I will have my chance at the west tower. He needs the vote of the entire cathedral chapter to end construction. He's just delaying, hoping to put it off until the best masons are hired elsewhere. Then he'll have a legitimate reason to do nothing this year." Master Raymond coughed, and then took a ragged breath. He paced again, three steps to the door, three steps back to the bed, three steps there, three steps back.

She sat back on the bed, out of his way, and pulled her blanket back around her shoulders. She didn't like that nagging cough, but Father already drank herbal tea with his supper, and after that, she could only wait for the return of warm weather and hope that it would cure his cough.

Now, Father's tirade continued: "And I've had word from the Quarry Master, too. If we don't order stone by the week's end, he will sell our stone to the friars of St. Assisi Monastery."

"Is there any hope?" She felt herself shrinking away from his anger and huddled under her blanket, pulling it over her head like a shawl.

"But the good Father forgets: I still have powerful friends who've never taken to this Southerner."

"Powerful friends?"

"Powerful enough." He pointed at her as if challenging her to find something wrong in his plan. "I'll talk to Father Colin tomorrow. You'll see. He will understand."

But the words sounded like a bluff to Laurel. She pulled her feet up to her chin and scooted back to lean against the wall. If only she could turn aside her father's words by ignoring them. She pulled the blanket tighter, burying her face in her knees. In a muffled voice, she repeated, "Is there any hope?"

"Have faith, daughter," Father said. "God uses the foolishness of man to accomplish his work."

She struggled to swallow, to speak, "But is there any hope?"

Father was silent. Instead, he came to sit beside her, and she turned and let him draw her into a hug. They were quiet for a moment, and then Laurel answered herself, her voice flat and hard, "It will take a miracle."

Father patted her shoulder awkwardly, "Then we will hope. For a miracle."

SEVEN

A fter a restless night, Laurel rose early. Her father still slept. Though his breathing was noisy, it was gentle, and that settled her worries about his cough. Quietly, she took her basket and slipped out into the crowded streets.

The townspeople were already busy fetching water, cooking breakfast and opening shops. Laurel paused for a moment watching the long shadows of the cathedral stretch across the western part of town and point to the hillsides beyond the walls. She wondered what she would find today. Had the Rovers found a good cave? Was Antonio healing?

Winding through the streets toward the city gate, Laurel was greeted often and affectionately by those she had recently tended: a small girl whose thumb still bore a bright red scar; the butcher's wife who sat in the sun, still weak after a fever last week; an old man who still walked with a cane after a broken leg at mid-winter. Each one called after her, "Going to see the Rovers? Be careful."

The whole town must know she was going to see the Rovers. Since Laurel had become the town's herbalist, she was often called on to doctor a fever or a nasty cut. What surprised her was how the town folk now watched out for her. And she was grateful for their concern.

She finally arrived at the city gates only to find them still shut. She leaned against a nearby house, waiting along with a few others who were up early and waiting to leave town.

Finally, the gatekeeper arrived. Edgar was the tallest man in town, thick-shouldered and sturdy. His speech was thick, too, hard to understand sometimes. Ignoring everyone, he went straight to the tall gates, unbolted them and heaved, digging his boots into the ground to lean hard and get the ponderous doors moving. When they were open, he stood aside and let the daily traffic start coming and going, entering and leaving Montague.

Laurel waved at Edgar and dodged the carts of farmers coming in. They had risen even earlier than she to be early at market. She stopped, though, at the sight of three magnificent white mares led by a bow-legged man.

Edgar called, "Ho! Horses! For who?"

"We seek Father Goossens."

"Horses for the Cardinal?" the gatekeeper asked.

The horseman nodded and moved on past Laurel.

Now the worry nagged at her again. Father Goossens was moving quickly on his plans for the Cardinal. There was little time to convince the cathedral chapter to build the west towers.

She and her father had lived all her life in Montague, in the upstairs tavern rooms which were paid for by the cathedral chapter. If he had to move to a new construction project, Father would likely go alone. He had already been talking about sending her to Dame Frances at her new home. Laurel had been afraid to show him her latest carvings, a Christ child small enough to fit in her palm. While Master Raymond bragged to the masons of her skills, he insisted that a mason's life wasn't meant for girls. He had already turned down three marriage proposals for her, but most girls married by thirteen or fourteen. She didn't want marriage and didn't want to move to a new town, a new cathedral. She didn't want anything to change.

Tired of the endless circle of her thoughts, Laurel shook her head and told herself to look around, to enjoy the beautiful spring morning. She turned into the forest path. The surrounding hills were riddled with caves, some shallow, some deep. Laurel strode through the woods where snow still lay in the shadows. She followed the wagon tracks and easily found where they had parked their wagon at the base of a gentle slope. Climbing up, she found a deep comfortable cave. She stamped her cold feet and shook snow from the bottom of her long black cape.

She waited in the entrance for her eyes to adjust to the half-light. "Hello?"

"Laurel! Thank you for coming." It was Ana-Maria, the Rover girl. They were probably about the same age, but Ana-Maria was slightly taller.

The cave was dry and warm, a sanctuary from the biting winds. Three beds of pine boughs were laid on narrow ledges a few feet off the ground. Ana-Maria had swept the area clean of small pebbles and other rubble. A nearby shelf overflowed with baskets and bundles, things brought up from the wagon.

Ana-Maria was stirring a pot over a smoky fire. A red shawl was slung lazily over her shoulders and her long black hair fell over it in waves.

"Jassy is out," she said. "He's clever at setting traps and catching something for the stew pot."

Laurel nodded toward the sleeping man. "How is Antonio?"

"Not good. He ran a fever all night."

Laurel's heart sank and she knelt beside Antonio. Blue veins stood out on his pale temple and scalp. She removed the damp cloth from his forehead and felt his face.

Too hot!

She pulled back the cover, exposing the wounded leg. It was an angry red; worse, a red streak ran up his leg toward his torso, definitely infected and definitely spreading fast. Sometimes it took days for an infection to spread, but sometimes it happened overnight like this. And when it was fast, it was often fatal. A shiver ran down her spine.

Laurel sat back on her heels and stared at the wound. To busy herself, she flipped through the cotton bags of herbs in her basket and felt how little remained in each. She remembered Dame Frances reciting the herbs she always carried. "Rue to clean a wound and lemon balm to dry up sores and wounds. Tansy and lemon balm tea for the fever. And never give mint to a wounded person because it would kill him for sure."

Laurel held up the lemon balm to her nose and breathed deeply, still avoiding the sight of Antonio's leg. She had small amounts of those herbs left, but this injury would use all she had. She'd have no more until plants in the wood started to grow again. While she wanted to save her meager store of herbs for the villagers, she couldn't refuse to help the old man.

Without being asked, Ana-Maria brought Laurel a bowl of hot water. Nodding to her, Laurel untied the herb bags and shook out the last of them into the bowl. With clean cloths that Ana-Maria handed her, Laurel washed the wound as well as she could. But she wasn't hopeful. It wasn't the outside that mattered; the infection was spreading inside.

"Save the rest of this to bathe him later," she instructed Ana-Maria.

The Rover girl covered the bowl with a clean cloth and set it aside.

"Will he be okay?" Jassy said from behind them. He handed Ana-Maria a white rabbit, which hung limp, its head cocked, its legs dangling.

Laurel debated, but realized they probably knew anyway. She rose and motioned Jassy and Ana-Maria back to the fire. With a low voice, she said, "It's infected. And with my herbs all gone, he may get worse."

Ana-Maria drew a sharp breath, but she quickly controlled it. Jassy rubbed a hand across his eyes, and then nodded. "We have no herbs left either. A fever went around our people this winter and our remedies were all used. Are there no herbs at the market in town?"

Laurel shook her head, "It was a sickly winter for many here, too."

For a moment, no one said anything. Laurel was suddenly aware of a heavy breathing behind her. She twisted around and saw the great bulk of the bear. He wore a leather collar with thick spikes. A short chain was fastened to the collar, and then to a metal ring that they had already embedded in rock. Another chain with a heavy ball was fastened to his rear foot. His breathing was shallow and noisy.

Laurel shuddered. The bear was placid, like a soft furry pillow. But he had slashed his master's leg, perhaps killed him.

Ana-Maria saw her glance and said, "The bear is gentle. He wouldn't hurt anyone."

"He's never attacked before?"

"Antonio found the bear when it was just a cub." Ana-Maria's voice was low and husky, a pleasant voice for storytelling or singing. "It was at a village far south of here where he spent the winter. Its mother was dead, killed by villagers who were angry that the bears were scaring their sheep. Antonio stopped them from killing the cub. He left the village that night and as the cub grew, he trained him

to dance. Named him Lucky because they always made
lots of money together."

"So, the bear repays the kindness by ripping his master's leg?" Laurel shook her head.

"That crowd was wild, you were there. Antonio should
have stopped the show. But then, he never would stop
until the crowd stopped throwing coins."

Laurel puzzled over that. Was it Jassy or Antonio who
had refused to stop? To risk your life for a few more
coins—it made no sense. She pulled a small bottle from
her basket.

"Give him sips of this mandrake wine when he wakes.
It will ease the pain."

"You're wrong. He won't die, you know." Ana-Maria bit
her lower lip and her eyes filled with tears. "Can he eat
anything?"

Laurel patted her shoulder, awkward, aware that anything she did was inadequate. "If you can get him to eat,
it could help. Who knows?"

Ana-Maria's dark eyes flashed, and her jaw clenched in
a stubbornness that was Antonio's only chance. She set
the mandrake wine beside the fire and said, "Rabbit stew.
Some good thick broth, that's what he needs. It will make
him stronger." She put on her cloak and picked up their
biggest pot. "I'll get water and be right back, Jassy."

She left, leaving Laurel and Jassy.

"And I must get back," Laurel said.

"Thank you again for your help," Jassy said. He walked her out to the cave's entrance.

Jassy gestured to the cathedral that was silhouetted in the eastern sky.

"Will they need extra workers this year? A bear-baiter's assistant is the only life I've ever known, but with Antonio sick—" He cleared his throat. "—if Antonio can't travel for a while, I will need work. I'd like to work on something like that, something that will still be here in a hundred years."

Laurel leaned against the cave wall and studied the strange young man. She guessed he was fourteen or fifteen. Dark bushy eyebrows shadowed a long nose. He wore a cream linen shirt, dark grey breeches with long woolen stockings, a wide black belt and comfortable black boots. Most travelers wore comfortable-looking boots; masons wore sturdy boots to protect their feet from construction accidents. Would he like switching boots?

It surprised her that they had so much in common. While she had the security of the cathedral all her life, she now faced losing that. He just wanted what she had always had. What would she do this year if they didn't build? Would she ever become a stone carver?

Father Goossens tolerated her constant presence only because of her father. If the construction didn't start, he would banish her except for the mass.

"No apprentices this year. Unless the Lord works a miracle,"—she raised her hands to the heavens in an appeal— "Father Goossens has decided there is no reason to build the west tower. Not this year, not ever." She tried to keep the bitterness from her voice.

Like her, Jassy still stared at the cathedral's shape on the horizon. "I don't understand. It's a magnificent cathedral. The best I've seen, and we've traveled far. I've seen grey, brown or yellow stones before, but never red. Nothing so beautiful as this."

She shrugged. "If you like, I can introduce you to Master Gimpel, the new carver. Perhaps he needs an assistant."

"Yes!"

"Come tomorrow, then. Ask an altar boy to find me. Now, I must get back."

"Again, I am in your debt," Jassy said. "If you ever need me, I will not hesitate to help."

Jassy's offer was comforting, somehow. She didn't know what a Rover boy would ever be able to do to help her, but it was more than she got from some of the town folk. "Thank you, Jassy. Your offer is kind and I will remember it."

And then, Laurel waved and wound down the hill, through the forest and back to the cathedral for the day's work.

EIGHT

....

L aurel spent the afternoon carrying statues and gargoyles down from the east tower. They should have worked on them in the upstairs workshop, but Master Gimpel decided he liked working on the ground floor of the cathedral, and with so few masons, her father and Father Goossens were inclined to oblige the master's whims. Moving one statue wasn't bad; moving the thirty-four statues that Master Gimpel wanted to work on first was a bone-weary task. She was glad he hadn't wanted all fifty-seven moved today.

Now, at dusk, Laurel shoved the wheelbarrow out of a muddy rut. The gargoyle inside bounced, but the straw pile cushioned it nicely. She stopped in front of the workshop and let the wheelbarrow handles drop. She shook out her arms, loosening up her muscles. She was tired, but she bent and slipped her arms around the statue and staggered over the threshold into the shop. Looking around, she was pleased with the statues lined up neatly on the worktables. Master Gimpel should be happy with her work, and maybe he would let her do some small pieces of carving. She put up the wheelbarrow and trudged back to the tavern for supper with Father.

The next morning, the cock's crow woke Laurel, and she found that her father was already gone for the day. Propped on one shelf was Father's drawing of the cathedral. Quickly she wrapped it with cloths again and carried it with her to the cathedral.

But Master Gimpel was in the workroom already.

Entering, Laurel barely glanced at the Gargoyle Man. Already his ugliness was becoming familiar and comfortable; even the eye patch seemed commonplace.

Without looking up from a chunk of grey marble, he said, "Thank you for bringing down the statues. Are they all in good shape?"

"All but one," Laurel said, pleased that he had noticed her work. "St. Francis has a chip on his robe. Small, but you should look at it."

The Gargoyle Man yawned and stretched and walked over to the statue of the Saint. She set Father's picture on her chosen worktable, and then joined him to look at the statue.

In this marble version of St Francis, he held a bird on his outstretched hand while a deer slept at his feet. Master Gimpel ran a hand over the sculpted face and down the stone robe. "Overall, good workmanship."

Of course, it was good craftsmanship, she thought. Master Benoit and her father would allow nothing shoddy in their workshops.

"You're right, his robe needs work," Master Gimpel said. "It's a small flaw, though. I can rework it and no one will know."

Laurel found his confidence aggravating, but she simply said, "Good."

"Go over the other statues again for any flaws," Master Gimpel said. He wiped his hands on his leatherwork apron, and then picked up the statue of St. Francis, carried it around to his worktable and set it beside his grey marble. He pulled a stool up to his workbench and eased onto the seat, favoring his bad leg. His thumb rubbed across the small flaw on St. Francis' robe, and he picked up a fine-grain rasp.

Without looking at Laurel, he asked. "What's that bundle you brought in? I run a tidy workshop; no trash lying about."

Laurel looked up from the statue she was inspecting for flaws. "Oh, I'll put it up." She scooted down the aisle to her corner where she had her own petite-sized tools, her own projects. Picking up Father's painting, she started to hide it under her bench.

"I didn't ask you to move it," Master Gimpel said. "I asked, 'What is it?'"

"It's nothing."

"Humph. Which means it's important." He hesitated, his forehead wrinkled, then said, "Ah. It's your father's drawing for the west tower. I understand that Father

Goossens saw it yesterday, but it failed to change his mind." He limped around to her corner. "Show me."

Laurel had no choice. With trembling hands, she unwrapped the framed picture.

Eagerly, the Gargoyle Man almost snatched the picture from her hands and carried it to where the workshop window was propped open letting in the soft spring day. He studied it for a full five minutes, while Laurel studied the emotions crossing his face and tried to guess his thoughts, something she could easily do for most of the townspeople. But his scarred face made it impossible to read him at all.

"This design is the work of a master!" He looked up and his surprisingly normal smile made Laurel blink. "And better than that, the turrets are perfect for gargoyles and statues. I will become the most famous gargoyle sculptor of all time, and your father will be the most famous architect. He's a genius."

Laurel's face flushed, like she had just been complimented instead of her father. Here was another ally, another who loved her cathedral. She didn't trust herself to speak.

"In spite of this–" He tapped the picture frame. "–they won't start building this year?"

His question loosed a flurry of anger. "No. And if we don't buy stone this year, there may not be stone left when we need it. Do you know who offers to buy our stone? The friars of St. Assisi. How could they do this?"

"Chapters change all the time," he continued. "It may take a year or two, but you'll be building here again soon. I've seen it happen many times."

"But my father—" She forced her voice to steady. "Father isn't a young man. If they wait, another architect may get to design the west tower. I pray for a miracle."

"You mean money?"

"Yes, money. But something to change Father Goossens's mind, too. Even with the money, he might decide to spend it elsewhere."

"Hmm. Difficult." The Gargoyle Man shook his head and went back to his own worktable. He sat. He turned the St. Francis statue around, and then around again. He looked over at Laurel.

Refusing to cry, Laurel reached for her herb basket that she carried everywhere. "Money to build isn't your problem. I shouldn't worry you. Do you mind if I sprinkle the workshop with herbs to make it smell better?"

"Go on," he waved a hand.

The strewing herbs weren't medicinal, so she had plenty left this spring. She liked a sweet smell to rooms she had to use often. She scattered the herbs on the rush floor and around her worktable where they would be stepped on and their odor released. Moving quietly so she wouldn't disturb him, she scattered more herbs around the Gargoyle Man's bench.

He was still turning St. Francis in a slow pirouette. Suddenly— "I know where you can get the money."

Laurel breathed deeply, the herbs filling the workshop with sweet incense. "A miracle?"

He laughed shortly. "Who knows? A miracle or a curse." Then his face pinched, tight with control. His scarred hands reached and flipped up his eye patch.

Like it was a mask he wanted to take off, Laurel thought. She shivered, suddenly scared. She stepped back, "No—"

But it was too late, the Gargoyle Man pried open his eyelid.

Despite herself, Laurel couldn't look away. Inside his eye socket was an eye. No, not an eye, for what lay inside was glittering.

He tugged at the thing and it came out with a soft sucking sound. Now his eyelid hung slack over the empty socket.

Her hand flew to her mouth and she gasped. She wanted to scream but couldn't find the breath.

But the Gargoyle Man was smiling now and holding out his palm. A ruby. Blood red. His voice gruff, he asked, "Have you ever seen a Troll's Eye?"

NINE

"**G**o on, take it." The Gargoyle Man cupped the red stone—the Troll's Eye—in his hand and held it out to Laurel.

She shuddered, feeling like a mouse trapped in the gaze of a snake.

"Take it," he commanded.

"It's a jewel?" Laurel gingerly took it between her thumb and forefinger–it was warm with the heat of his body–and held it at arm's length. Just the thought of it was repulsive. Yet the red stone gleamed invitingly. It was a large oval, about one inch long and three quarters of an inch wide. The deep ruby red was broken by a red-black slit in the center, like the pupil of a cat's eye.

"It is beautiful. In—in a way," Laurel stuttered. "B-but one jewel won't pay for the building."

The Gargoyle Man's arms were crossed over his chest. "I won't part with it anyway. But it can lead you to a treasure cave that has enough jewels to finance a hundred west towers."

"What?"

"This isn't a plain gemstone. It's a Troll's Eye, a doorway into secret lands. Trolls are creatures of the mountains and have more understanding of stone than even we masons. After my apprenticeship with Giselbertus, I spent a year searching out stone lore of the trolls. I traveled far, far north and found many tales of their ways with stone. They have found a way to enter the worlds that are within stone. Each block in this cathedral has a world within in. The trolls call these worlds the *Djuber*, which means *The Deep*. It is in these lands that trolls hide their treasure. Look!" He took the jewel from her and held it against the blood-red stone they had unloaded the day before. He reminded Laurel of a child showing off a prize.

A jewel as a doorway? A treasure cave? He wasn't just ugly, he was moonstruck, a lunatic. She shook her head and took another step backward, making sure she could dash out the doorway if needed.

"Ah, I see. You talk of miracles, but you don't believe."

Laurel frowned. She tilted her head and watched the jewel twinkle in the light. Something wasn't right here. "Why are you so anxious for me to look through it?"

"It won't hurt," he shrugged. "I promise."

Laurel bent over, glancing at the Gargoyle Man as she did so. He was quite still, waiting, almost as if he was afraid he would spoil the moment if he moved. And her suspicion overcame her curiosity. She straightened. "No."

Master Gimpel straightened up and took the Troll's Eye away from the red stone. Casually, he tossed the jewel up and down while he studied her. "When you are willing to look for a miracle, talk to me again. Meanwhile—

Child—take the drawing back to your father. There's a good little girl."

Laurel gritted her teeth, angry at this ugly monster of a mason who thought he could come in and take over the workshops and force her to trudge up the eastern tower steps and then down again, carrying statues that weighed as much as she did. Thirty-four trips she had made yesterday afternoon, while he just sat and sharpened chisels. Thirty-four heavy stone statues she had carried. She had worked hard to get this workshop in order. And now, he was treating her like a child. No!

As the jewel fell toward his hand, she snatched it.

She would look through his Troll's Eye.

"Laurel!" Ana-Maria bustled through the open doorway. She shaded her eyes, trying to adjust to the dim interior. "You must come. Antonio is worse. He needs something to calm him."

Master Gimpel flipped his eye patch into place, and then gripped Laurel's hand and squeezed, forcing her to drop the jewel into his hand. He clutched it, hiding it from view, and stepped back toward the deeper shadows.

"Ana-Maria!" Laurel was confused, turning back and forth between the man and girl. "Um. This is the new mason, Master Gimpel. Master, may I go? We have no doctor in our town, so I do what I can with herbs. Her master's leg is infected."

With a soft, gentle voice, he said, "Of course, you must go and help." To Ana-Maria, he said, "Wait outside a moment and she will come."

She nodded and stepped outside.

Waiting until the Rover girl was looking away from the workshop, the Gargoyle Man gripped Laurel's shoulders and whispered fiercely: "The Troll's Eye is a secret. You must tell no one."

Laurel chewed on her inner cheek.

"No one," he insisted.

She shrugged off his hands and glared.

The Gargoyle Man lifted the eye patch, opened his palm and slid the Troll's Eye back into the eye socket. He blinked.

Laurel recoiled, stumbling backward. The stone twinkled, like it was a real eye, an evil eye. She couldn't tell if he could see through it or not. He adjusted the eye patch and it disappeared, leaving just his scarred face, now smiling at her.

How silly of her. Of course, he couldn't see anything through a stone. He took her cloak off the peg by the doorway, draped it over her shoulders and motioned outside.

As she passed him, he laid a finger on his lips. "Remember, no one."

TEN

L aurel and Ana-Maria hurried through the town. The snow was slushy from the warm weather and their skirt hems were muddy. Laurel stopped by her lodgings to search for any remnants of herbs that she might have overlooked. Of twelve different herbs, she was out of ten. Of the other two, she had only pinches left. After a moment's hesitation, she added a bottle of mandrake wine to her basket.

The warm weather had brought everyone outside, crowding the streets with jovial throngs. The two girls wove through the marketplace as quickly as they could and on to the town gates.

"How is the old Rover?" called Edgar, the gatekeeper.

"Not good," Laurel answered.

"Be careful of those Rovers!" the gatekeeper called.

Laurel glanced at Ana-Maria, but she seemed to not hear the gatekeeper, or else she chose not to hear him.

The girls walked swiftly through the woods toward the cave. Sunlight glittered off the snow, almost blinding Laurel. She had almost looked through the Troll's Eye because the Gargoyle Man had tantalized her with the promise of a treasure. No, he had charmed her, like a magician doing tricks so that she had almost looked through his jewel. In fact, a jewel that allowed you to enter a stone world had—for a moment—seemed the most reasonable thing in the world. Only Ana-Maria's arrival had saved her.

At the cave entrance, Laurel turned for a last look at the cathedral guarding the town. "Father's tower turrets do need to be built, though. And I do need a miracle," she whispered to herself. If Master Gimpel offered another chance to look through the Troll's Eye, would she risk it in hopes of finding a treasure?

She entered the cave, and for a moment, she thought she had entered the cathedral: there was a high dome ceiling, dim light, deep quiet, and stone enveloping her. But elegant cut stone was replaced by crude untutored stone. Cathedral incense was supplanted by the stale cave air and smoke from the cook fire.

A moan cut through her confusion.

Jassy rubbed bleary eyes and ran a hand through tangled hair. "He's worse."

Laurel touched his shoulder. "Go rest. I'll take care of Antonio."

"Later. First, tell us how he is doing."

Ana-Maria said hopefully, "We've been bathing him in spring water and the herb water you left."

Laurel knelt beside Antonio and touched his cheek. Burning hot. She studied the slash on his leg. Now the angry red had spread up and down his leg, the infection taking hold. For Antonio's sake, she was glad they weren't in a dark, suffocating chamber. If she had herbs, well, she might bring the fever down, might control the infection. Bathing him with cool water was all they could do now.

She looked up at Jassy and Ana-Maria and shook her head.

Jassy turned away and pulled Ana-Maria with him. "I told you Laurel had no more herbs."

Ana-Maria hid her face in his shoulder, and they stood together in sorrow.

Seeing Jassy comforting the girl, Laurel turned away in pity. She knelt beside Antonio and poured a cup of mandrake wine. Gently, she held up Antonio's head and tried to help him drink. She forced her hands to be steady, gentle. Some wine dribbled down Antonio's chin, but some managed to go into his mouth. When he had swallowed about half a cup, enough to help him sleep a while, she settled him back onto his pallet. She stood awkwardly, trying not to look at the Rovers.

Ana-Maria stepped away from Jassy and took Laurel's hands in hers. "Antonio is the only family I have. Please help him."

Clearing her throat, Laurel said, "My old nurse taught me herbs, and I try. But I can't perform miracles."

Solemnly, Laurel kissed Ana-Maria's cheek. They dropped hands. Ana-Maria pulled on both ends of her shawl and tied them together. Then, she picked up a rag, soaked it in a bucket of water, wrung it out and bent to bath Antonio's pale face.

Jassy motioned Laurel to the cave entrance.

Searching for something to say, Laurel asked, "What will you do?"

Jassy looked back at Antonio. "You mean if Antonio doesn't make it?" He cleared his throat. "Here in the dark cave, the bear is drowsy. As the weather warms, though, he'll be restless. Still, we may have a few more weeks of quiet."

"Where will you go?"

Jassy rubbed his eyes, and then and looked over the countryside. His voice was almost plaintive: "In search of our fortunes."

"Fortunes? You mean your destiny? Or riches?"

"Maybe both."

Laurel caught her breath with a sudden hope. Maybe Jassy would go with her into the stone world and search for his fortunes there. Then she wondered: With his travel experience, maybe he'd heard something about Troll's Eyes and would know if they were dangerous. But, no. She had promised not to tell anyone about the jewel.

"The new mason is looking for one apprentice. He said you could come by and talk to him."

Jassy's tired face lit up, transformed by his sudden smile. Laurel realized how exhausted he really was. He must have slept little in the last few days.

He swept into a graceful bow. "I am in your debt, once more."

Despite herself, her voice was harsh, "Do you mean that?"

Jassy nodded, and then studied her face.

Promise or not, she needed advice. Still hesitant, she said, "What if I told you I knew where there was a cave full of treasure?"

"I explored one or two caves around here—nothing else to do. Only sleeping bats."

Laurel's face flushed. "Not here. In a different place."

"Where?"

With a deep breath, Laurel blurted, "Through a Troll's Eye."

"Troll's Eye!" Ana-Maria emerged from the shadows.

Laurel blushed with anger. Ana-Maria was eavesdropping. Telling Jassy about the stone was bad enough. Still, she had to know more. "You've heard of them?"

Ana-Maria nodded. "I haven't seen one, though. Antonio and I traveled alone for one summer before Jassy joined us. It was a hot summer to the south and Antonio liked to stay cool. We traveled farther and farther north searching for cool weather. The north country is a strange land where days are long and nights are short and it is always cool. Many strange tales did I hear that summer. Would you hear of the Troll's Eye?"

"Yes!" Laurel settled onto a large boulder and Jassy squatted nearby.

Ana-Maria stood in front of them, dramatically silhouetted in the cave opening. Her husky voice was compelling: "Know then that in the northern lands there are trolls, wicked creatures that live in the mountains. They travel abroad only at night and scamper back to their caves by dawn. If one should happen to be late, the sun's rays turn them to stone. They hate the long summer days, days of confinement for them.

"We met a hermit, an old man who lived alone, who said he had found a troll which had been turned to stone. Its eyes gleamed like jewels. He pried out one of the red jewels and looked through it."

Ana-Maria picked up a stone from the cave floor and put it to her eye. She peered around with the stone eye. Jassy half-smiled at her play.

"And?" Laurel urged. It wasn't play to her.

"The hermit said when he looked through the Troll's Eye, he was cursed, and everything was reversed: crude was fine, ugly was beautiful, and bad was good. 'Beware the Troll's Eye,' he said."

Ana-Maria hefted the stone and threw it far into the woods. "Beware the Troll's Eye!" She turned on heel and strode back to Antonio.

Laurel bent her head and shivered.

But Jassy took off his hat and held it out to her. "She's a great storyteller, isn't she? She could make money even without the bear."

Frustrated, Laurel brushed away his cap.

He put it back on his curls. "I never know where she gets her stories. Makes them up, I guess."

"You don't believe the story?" Laurel asked.

"It's just a story."

Laurel bit her bottom lip. Was it a story?

He waited. When she said nothing, he leaned closer, his whole body suddenly alert: "You're serious! You've really seen a Troll's Eye?"

"I don't know if it came from one of those troll creatures, but I've seen a gemstone that looks like an eye. And, no, I didn't look through it." *I would have, though, if Ana-Maria hadn't stopped me,* she thought guiltily.

Impatient, Jassy waved his hand in small circles to speed up her answer. "Where? Who has it?"

But she was slow to answer. "The new mason is—odd. You'll see when you meet him." She didn't want to tell anyone about the gemstone, but who else would believe her? The townspeople? The priests? Her father? No, she had to trust these Rovers. "Master Gimpel has the jewel and says it's like a doorway to another world. He said a treasure cave is inside a stone that he owns."

Jassy stood abruptly and shook his head. "Then why doesn't he go and get the treasure?"

"I don't know. But I want to know more about this Troll's Eye—curse or no curse. We need money to build this year and a treasure cave would solve everything."

From inside the cave, Ana-Maria called again, "Beware the Troll's Eye."

And from the depths of the cave, the bear growled in his sleep, the sound echoing throughout the cave.

ELEVEN

Above the cathedral spires, early afternoon clouds were gathering, building higher. A brisk wind picked up, rustling the trees and warning of a spring storm.

"I must get back," Laurel said.

"I'll walk you back to the city gates." Jassy caught up his red cloak and a staff and led the way.

At first the woods were eerily quiet, as if waiting for the storm. But as the storm drew nearer, the wind sharpened and reached even the forest floor. Bare branches rustled. Laurel shivered, drawing her cloak closer and pulling up her hood. Then they passed into a valley where dark pines and firs nestled and the wind could barely reach. The early spring sun couldn't penetrate here either, so the snow lay thicker and chunks fell into her boot tops as she struggled through it, leaving her feet wet and cold. Laurel peered around the edge of her hood at Jassy, but he was hooded, too. They walked as if alone, both intent on stamping through the snow.

Then Laurel heard a shuffling or scraping noise.

And a figure came into view.

Jassy lunged through a drift to put himself between the figure and Laurel. Cautious, Laurel stepped behind a fir and watched.

Slide, step. Pause. Slide, step. Pause.

Jassy twirled his staff and called out, "Hold!"

That gait seemed familiar, was it—?

The figure stopped, but Jassy charged with a roar.

"Jassy!" Laurel called, trying to stop him. "It's Master Gimpel, the mason."

Jassy faltered and stopped, looking back at Laurel and then at the hooded man.

Laurel's heart pounded. Oddly, she could only think of Master Gimpel's hood: she was glad he wore his hood up, throwing his face into deep shadow. Otherwise Jassy might not have stopped at her call.

The older man cleared his throat and gave a short bow to Jassy. To Laurel, he called, "You left so quickly, I was worried. Snowstorms, wolves and such."

"My father allows me to come and go as the nursing requires. Besides, I have an escort," she said shortly.

When the mason said nothing, she remembered her manners. "This is Jassy. Jassy, this is Master Gimpel."

"I thought the Rover was an old man," said Master Gimpel.

Laurel blew out a breath and shifted her herb basket to her left arm. "One of them is. Antonio is burning with fever." She rubbed her face with her free hand and tried to shake off the memory of Antonio's wound.

Master Gimpel nodded, and then asked Jassy, "So, you're the young rover. And when your master dies?"

Jassy raised an eyebrow at Laurel; she nodded encouragement.

"Laurel says you need an apprentice."

"Mistress Raymond is correct."

Laurel chaffed at the formal use of her name, the implied criticism of her friendship with Jassy. She didn't mind that Jassy called her Laurel.

"Let me see your hands." Master Gimpel took Jassy's hands and turned them over. "Long fingers." Still without looking up, he said, "Why do you want to work with stone?"

Jassy's voice was quiet, uncertain. "The stones call to me."

"Ah, you've heard them?" Master Gimpel sounded surprised. "Good. Very good. Then come tomorrow at dawn. I'll try you out and see if you have any feel for stone or if you just hear them."

Jassy shook the mason's hand. "Thank you, sir. Dawn. I'll be there."

But Laurel wasn't finished. "One more thing." She spoke quickly before she lost her nerve. "I've told Jassy about the Troll's Eye."

A blast of wind swept through the valley, shaking trees and dumping snow onto Laurel and Jassy. She shook it off, and when she looked up at the mason, she stepped backward.

He still stood fully cloaked, but he had stiffened, straightened. Stilled. Through gritted teeth, he said, "I said, tell no one."

Laurel straightened herself, defiant. "I needed advice."

Jassy stepped closer to Laurel, again making sure he was between her and the mason. He thrust his staff upright into a snowdrift and leaned against it, his dark eyes even darker. "And I have questions about this Troll's Eye. Why don't you go through it and find the treasure yourself?"

The mason seemed to hesitate, and then sighed and relaxed. He glanced around till he saw a fallen log and limped over to sit on it, as if settling in for a long discussion. He spoke from the depths of his hood: "Ah, there are rules, every magic has rules."

Fascinated, Laurel started to join him on the log, but Jassy stopped her with a glance. She heeded the warning and stopped beside him. But she couldn't stop Jassy's questions.

"How do you know these rules?"

The mason whistled softly. "Some I learned by listening to legends about trolls, some I learned by breaking a rule."

Again, Laurel almost stepped closer, but Jassy held out his arm to stop her. "So. Tell us the rules of the Troll's Eye."

Shrugging, the mason said, "Of course. The Troll's Eye only lets a person enter a stone one time. Then you must try a different stone. I've already been to the treasure cave once and can't return."

"Then you brought back jewels?" Laurel stamped her feet from the cold, but also from frustration that the mason was being so guarded in his answers.

"No. My—well, my companion—he was injured, so I had to leave my bag of jewels to help him. Unfortunately—" He paused as if considering his next words carefully, "—the other one didn't make it."

A shiver went down Laurel's spine. "What do you mean?"

"I buried him in the stone world."

Laurel stammered, "Then—it's dangerous. There is a curse."

"Miracles don't come easily."

Now a cold fist of fear settled in Laurel's stomach and she started shivering. She clutched at her cloak and stamped her feet again.

Jassy kept his eyes on the mason. "Go on. What other rules?"

The mason chuckled. "The rules won't matter in the end. You will go through the Troll's Eye."

"Maybe," Jassy said harshly. "But we still need to know. Tell us the worst."

"Very well. When you go through the Troll's Eye, you must first find the right path. If you do, it will lead directly to the treasure cave. You must enter the cave only during the night when the Hallvard, the guardian of the treasure, sleeps. Ah—the treasure! Heaps and mounds of jewels of every color, just waiting for you." Master Gimpel waved his hands and scooped up imaginary treasure.

Laurel felt a thrill start to thaw her frozen senses. Treasure. They could build this year.

But the mason continued, "There are difficulties with the treasure, too. You may each take one bag of jewels." He held both hands out, palms up, and pretended to weigh something on a scale. "The trolls can't count. Instead, they weigh out their jewels. The treasure cave has a set of scales and weights and bags to carry jewels. You may take one Troll's Weight of jewels. It's the smallest of their weights, and it's heavy for a person to carry."

"They allow just anyone to take jewels?"

Master Gimpel shook his head. "It is said that dragons count each jewel, but trolls aren't as smart. They can't count. They only know the weight of stones in their hands." Now he waggled a finger at them. "But beware: if you take even one extra gemstone out of the treasure cave, the Hallvard will know. He will not allow you to leave his lands until he recovers all the jewels you have taken."

"What if we return the extra stone to the cave later? Or what if we put it in the bag later? Or—"

"Ah, you want to play a game of 'what if'? No, it doesn't work that way. When you leave the cave, the Hallvard knows what you carry. One extra gemstone, one stone more than a Troll's Weight bag—step foot outside the cave, and he will never stop hunting you."

"Hallvard?" Laurel asked with a shiver.

"It is a Norse word, from the land of the trolls. It means 'guardian of the rock'."

"One bag of jewels would be enough," Laurel said. "More than enough to build the west tower."

"What does this Hallvard look like?" Jassy asked.

The mason shrugged. "I don't know what manner of beast he is in truth, but he looks much like a bear. He is simply the Hallvard. He sleeps at night. But even by day, he won't bother you unless you take too many jewels."

The mason paused, but Jassy urged him on. "What other rules?"

"One day's walk in, one day's walk out, and one extra day," Master Gimpel continued. "The Troll's Eye will stay open three days. If you're not out by sunset on the third day, you'll be trapped forever."

Laurel laughed. "Sounds too easy."

"Sounds too dangerous," Jassy said.

They grinned at each other.

"You do the worrying," Laurel said. "I'll try to enjoy the journey."

Jassy thumped his staff up and down in the snowdrift. "When you travel, there are often surprises." He nodded toward the mason. "Anything else?"

The black hood nodded. "One more warning: however many go in, that same number must come out. If three go in, three must come out. If two go in, two must come out. One might get out alone, but not without paying a price."

"You mean, if there's an accident, and one is hurt and can't get back, then both are trapped? But your friend died there and here you are." Jassy's black eyebrows knit together, as if trying to understand.

Master Gimpel stood now and stepped toward Jassy and Laurel. Jassy held out his staff to protect Laurel but let the mason approach. The light was dusky under the trees. Casually, the mason threw back his hood and slowly turned to show his scarred face.

"Oh!" Jassy jerked backward. Then, as if pulled by a magnet, he stepped closer to the Gargoyle Man. "What? How?"

To Laurel, the man's face was another blast of cold air, and she started shivering again, tucking her hand under her armpits and stamping, avoiding that face. Shivering, but she didn't know if it was from cold or fear.

In the snowbound silence, the Gargoyle Man's words were eerie. "I wasn't born this way. During my trip into the Troll's Eye, my companion fell off a waterfall and I buried him beside the water. When I came back alone through the Troll's Eye, it left me scarred." He smiled broadly, and the effect was startling, transforming evil to a comforting face.

Laurel found herself smiling back.

"But there's no reason," the mason said, "to think you would have problems. In fact, there's one more treasure you might want to seek. In *Djuber*, the land of the Troll's Eye, you must look for an herb that grows there, and only there. It might help the old man. It's a vine, a small, star-shaped white flower that grows on rock walls. Pick the flowers and bring them back to dry. I don't know herbs, but my companion once told me this plan will cure infections."

Eagerly, Jassy said, "It would cure Antonio?"

The mason shrugged. "I don't know herbs, only what my friend told me."

From somewhere in the woods came the caw of a crow.

The mason held his hands out wide. "So, do you mean to try the Troll's Eye or not?"

Jassy shrugged. "It sounds like a profitable adventure."

"No. Never!" Laurel blurted.

"There's no rush," crooned the mason. "Go whenever you're ready."

"Never," she repeated. But her heartbeat thumped in her ears. The Troll's Eye would be there, tempting her. "Never." She said it louder, and it sounded false even to her. "Never," she whispered.

Master Gimpel flipped up his hood. His voice was smooth, soothing. "When you're ready. Now. Jassy, meet me at the workshop at dawn and we'll see how you like stone. Come to the workshop on the south side. I'll tell the gatekeeper to let you enter town early." He stepped forward, and before either could say anything, he took Laurel's herb basket from her arm. "Here. I'll carry that."

"No. Jassy will—"

"No arguing, now." He strode off, dragging his left foot and leaving a distinctive track through the snow.

Laurel looked at Jassy, who glanced back up the mountain toward his cave. He was worrying about Antonio, Laurel guessed.

"I can go with Master Gimpel," she said quickly.

Jassy hesitated, looking after the limping figure. "Are you sure?"

Laurel nodded decisively. "I'll see you tomorrow." Then she turned and trudged after the mason, following him up and out of the dreary valley, without looking back. Once on level ground, Laurel insisted on taking her basket back. "I'll hurry on ahead, if you don't mind," she said.

The mason nodded and continued his slow limp back toward town.

Laurel hurried, almost running through the growing twilight. One thing she vowed: if she ever did travel through a Troll's Eye, it wouldn't be alone. None of the townsfolk or the priests would do. It had to be Jassy. She needed his experience in traveling.

She shoved away the memory of the mason's scarred face. For three days, the Troll's Eye was open. Surely, that was enough time. Pulling her hood closer, Laurel brushed a stray hair from her forehead. And the thought came: Master Gimpel would have been a handsome man without the scars. Her fingers crept to her face and felt the familiar eyes, nose, and cheek.

She dropped her hands and dashed through the town gates, waving at Edgar, but not stopping at his questions. She raced through the streets and didn't stop until she reached the inn, just as fat raindrops started to fall.

She stamped the mud and snow from her boots and rushed in. Symon, the innkeeper, bustled forward, wiping his hands on his apron. "Mistress Laurel! Master Raymond has been worried. Hurry on up. I'll bring supper in a few minutes."

She nodded and trudged upstairs. The weary day suddenly descended on her. She had been early to the workshop and then walked out to the cave and back. Each step felt like lifting yet another statue. All Laurel wanted was a good night's sleep.

....

TWELVE

"Laurel! At last!" Her father's face was pale, drawn.

She stepped in and kissed his leathery cheek.

"How is Antonio?" Father Colin sat at the table beside the window. He had been the acting head of the cathedral chapter before Father Goossens had been brought in to take over. Father Colin was broad-shouldered priest, yet for a man of his size, he moved with a comforting gentleness.

"Not good. You should visit him before it's too late. The trail of the Rover wagon is easy to follow," Laurel said, suddenly guilty that she had not thought of this earlier.

"That bad? Yes, I'll find the cave tomorrow," he said. Then he rose and offered the chair to Laurel.

"No, I'll sit here." Laurel sank onto the bed and tugged off her boots. She wiggled her cold toes and sighed in relief. Still bent over, she dragged the boots to the fire and returned to the bed. All she wanted to do was lay down and sleep. But it was too quiet.

Looking up, both men were watching her.

"What's wrong?" she asked sharply.

Master Raymond clutched the edge of the table and leaned toward her. "My drawing. It's missing."

For a moment, she didn't understand. Then she remembered that she had taken his new drawing of the cathedral with her that morning. Was it only that morning? The day had been so full it seemed like months ago. She yawned. "I took it to the workshop. I wanted to study it while I worked."

They both stared at her.

"What?" Laurel demanded and looked anxiously from one to the other.

Father Colin patted her shoulder. "We meant to send it to the Cardinal today. We want to appeal directly to him with the plans. We think we might persuade him to allow construction to continue. When it was missing, we worried— "

She understood instantly, "—that Father Goossens had taken it again. He knows you want to go over his head to another authority." There were certainly enough gossips among the priests, so Father Goossens likely knew everything Father was doing. "I'm sorry. I meant to bring it back, but the Rovers needed me." She sighed and dropped her face to her hands.

"Laurel, I've been so worried." Her father turned to Father Colin. "The corner workshop, the one that Master Gimpel has started to use. Look there."

Chapter politics again, one cleric against another. Laurel closed her eyes and rubbed her temple. Why couldn't they just build? It was for God's glory. Didn't they see that?

Father Colin nodded at Master Raymond, "I'll go now and find it."

As he stepped out, Symon appeared with steaming bowls of lentil soup and a loaf of bread. Weary, Laurel barely managed to finish eating before she wrapped herself in a blanket and slept.

Sometime later, in the dead of the night, she woke suddenly. From the stable yard below came the soft whicker of a horse. Then, from inside the room, a cough.

Laurel leaned up on her elbow. Small slivers of moonlight filtered through the window shutters. Master Raymond sat on the edge of his bed.

He coughed again, one hack after the other, until it deepened into a racking cough that made his chest heave.

Laurel jumped from her bunk and quickly lit a candle. When the coughing continued, she thumped his back, hoping to dislodge something. "Your cough is worse!"

His thin body shook with each blow, but she kept at it until eventually the coughing spluttered out, leaving her father sagging and wheezing. In the candlelight, she saw that the gray of his beard now sprinkled his temples, and his face looked leaner, his nose sharper than she'd ever noticed.

"Father, sit." She ushered him to the edge of the lower bed where he sat hunched. "You should be over that cough by now."

He waved his hand, as if swatting away the question. "It's just a cold."

Hope flooded through her. Just a cold. "Be still and I'll make some tea."

But then he coughed again and this time, he dug under his pillow and pulled out a rag. He muffled the sound of his cough with the rag, and then dabbed at his mouth. The rag came away dark. He was spitting up blood.

"Father!" A deep despair clutched at her and she fought it by throwing her arms around him.

"There, there, child. There's nothing you can do." Awkwardly, he stroked her hair. His beard was scratchy, and he smelled like the incense burned in the cathedral. "I didn't want you to know."

She could barely force the words, "How long?"

"I've been coughing up blood for maybe a month." He didn't sound scared, just matter-of-fact.

It was stone dust. Dame Frances always said, "Stone masons leave their youth and health in the quarry." When one became sick, she left herbals. But Laurel had never known the herbals to do more than relieve the cough for an hour or so. As master architect, Master Raymond avoided much of the stone dust, but he still made frequent trips to the quarry. Stone dust was affecting him slower than it did the masons, but it had just caught up to him. She should have suspected this. No, she told herself fiercely, it's just a chest cold.

Laurel spun away to the fireplace, stirring up a fire and setting a small kettle to boil. Their lodgings—paid for by the cathedral chapter—were directly over the kitchen, so they had a tiny fireplace that vented into the main fire-place, the only inn room so lucky. As long as she could remember, this simple room had been home. Laurel and her father ate all their meals in the dining room, and Symon's maids cleaned their rooms, which relieved Maser Raymond from any domestic chores and left him free for his work.

Though they ate in the dining room most days, they did have two mugs and two spoons for the odd times like this. Laurel rummaged in her herbals basket, but there was only mint. No tansy to help him sleep.

Laurel dropped a generous pinch of crushed pepper-mint leaves into a square of coarse linen and tied twine around each sachet. She filled two mugs with steaming water and dropped in the mint to steep.

Then, she gritted her teeth against a sudden fear: he had been coughing up stone dust for a month! She leaned over to catch the pungent steam and breathed deeply, try-ing to calm herself.

When her father coughed again, she winced, but re-fused to look at his rag. It did not have blood on it, she tried to tell herself. It was only a cold.

She padded to the fireplace and realized her feet were frozen in the cold room. She raised her toes, letting the fire warm them. But nothing could defrost the fear that now held her.

Forcing a smile, she picked up Father's mug. "Drink. It will help you sleep."

If only miracles could really happen, she thought.

He curled bony fingers around the cup and breathed deeply before taking a sip. "I'm not afraid."

"I am."

"Father Colin will take you to Dame Frances."

"Don't."

"I must—"

"No! Just drink. Tomorrow. We can talk then. Not now."

He dropped his eyes to the cup and sighed. Then he blew on the hot tea, rippling the surface, and took a noisy sip. A cough caught him, and he held the cup away to keep spilling it on himself. When the cough passed, he sipped again, and then closed his eyes and let the steam warm his cheeks. By now the tea was cooler, so he took a longer drink and another until the mug was empty. At last, Laurel helped her father lay back down. The tea worked: his breathing grew regular, and he slept.

Wanting some comfort herself, Laurel picked up her stone bird, the tiny gargoyle her father had given her. She dragged the stiff chair from the window to the fireplace. Pulling up her legs, she wrapped a blanket around her shoulders and clutched the bird to her chest. The flames burned yellow and orange; a red coal flared briefly, like a door opening and shutting. Is that how the Troll's Eye would look when it opened and shut? She had no choice now. Besides the money to build the cathedral, her father needed a miracle and he needed it now.

At last, Laurel crawled into bed and fell into a restless sleep. She dreamed of a gargoyle with flower petals cascading from a bag on his back. The flower scent poured over his face, burying him with a heavy, sweet odor. Then he was screaming: "Let me out! I repent!" But there was no escaping from the solid stone.

Laurel woke in a panic, fighting covers and gasping for breath.

"Let me out! Let me out!" she screamed silently. Pulling the covers off her face, she breathed deeply and tried to calm down.

And then she found herself out of bed, staring at her father. But there was no comfort there. She pulled on her shoes, wrapped a shawl over her head and trudged through the muddy streets to the cathedral. She shoved open a heavy side door and entered. Darkness enveloped her, but she knew her way. Like a blind man, she knew the exact number of shallow steps that wound up, around the outside of the east tower. One hand trailed the wall. Already the smooth walls and the rhythmic walk up the steps had a calming effect. After fifty-seven steps, she turned left and found the door to the sculpture room.

Moonlight streamed in through two windows onto the mounds of hay that had covered the remaining statues. She stretched out, pillowing her head on a Saint Stephen—the patron saint of stonemasons—and tucked her feet between two long-necked gargoyles whose twisted faces were comforting in their familiarity. She sighed in relief—home, at last. Now, she could sleep.

··

THIRTEEN

L aurel was up before dawn and back home before Father woke. Quietly, she tied a couple new sachets of peppermint and left them for Master Raymond's breakfast. She looked around the familiar room, wondering what she should take on her journey and decided to pack just her stone bird, and a change of clothing. She didn't know what else she would need.

There were many questions to answer: should she explain to her father that she would be gone for a couple days? Would she have to convince Jassy to go with her? When could they leave? She needed fast answers. There was no time to waste.

She was back outside—a fine mist was falling now, a gentle spring rain—and at the oak cathedral doors in time for the hour of lauds, the early prayers scheduled for the hour before dawn. She shoved the cathedral doors, and when they gave way, she stumbled, almost falling into the nave. She shook rain off her cape and threw back her hood. Then, she stilled, letting the peace, the quiet of the cathedral wash over her.

Under a long row of arches, a cleric strode sedately toward the altar. His dim lantern measured his progress, pace by pace. He lit the candles in the large candelabra one by one, slowly chasing away the cave-like darkness.

The nave usually looked solemn and spare to Laurel. Now, great shadows from the candelabra, the wooden pews, and the arches gave the room a sudden opulence that startled her. She was pleased she had come to early prayers, pleased the cathedral could still surprise her.

Staying near the back, Laurel bent her head in prayer and let the cathedral wrap her with peace. The untutored quarry stone had been taught to pray by the touch of talented masons. Like other pilgrims before her, Laurel prayed with the hope that her needs would reach the heavens: prayers for Master Raymond's healing, for Antonio's healing and for a successful trip through the Troll's Eye. Prayers for courage to make the trip.

The first rays of sunlight shot through the stained-glass windows far above her and suddenly the ceiling glowed as if she was looking into the gates of heaven itself. A good omen. Yes, she could go through the Troll's Eye. She *would* go. The light meant it was dawn and the skies were clearing.

She wondered if her father was awake yet, wanting, needing a brew of herbs and not finding her, thinking she was downstairs in the tavern kitchen or out tending to someone. If she and Jassy went through the Troll's Eye today—and she hoped they would—tomorrow would be even worse for her father.

Slipping her hand into her pocket, she found and clutched her stone gargoyle bird, glad she had brought something familiar with her. She should hurry, or she'd be late to meet Jassy, but somehow haste seemed inappropriate inside the cathedral. Years slid by as she watched the candles burn shorter. The sun slept daily within the tiles, the moldings, the columns, the stone arches. The sun's rays were daily woven into netting that trapped and slowed time. The cathedral would live for centuries.

A cleric stopped beside her. "Daughter, why do you weep?"

She hadn't known she was crying. "I don't know."

The cleric raised an eyebrow, puzzled. He hesitated a moment longer and then strode on.

And Laurel whispered, "Because I need a miracle. And I'm scared of what a miracle might cost me."

She rose from prayers and went to the door. But she stopped to turn around, to lean her back against the rosy stone and commit the sight to memory. Then she squared her shoulders and whispered to the cathedral, "I hope."

FOURTEEN

....

J assy stood in the doorway of the workshop, wearing sturdy boots and his thick but ragged red cloak. At his feet was a pack. He looked rested, better than his haggard face of yesterday. Somehow, he had managed to sleep, which was more than she had managed except for the short time in the workroom.

She took his hands and pulled him aside.

"What's wrong?" he asked.

Her voice shook as she explained her father's illness. "He won't last another year," she ended.

Jassy lifted her chin until their eyes met. "You're going inside the Troll's Eye," he said flatly. "And you want me to go with you."

Laurel held her breath, waiting for his answer. She would beg if she had to. No, she wouldn't try to trick him with emotions. Either he would go or not. But–oh! –she didn't want to go alone.

"Yes, I'll go. I told you that we repay our debts and we are at least twice indebted to you for taking care of Antonio."

"You're sure?"

"Yes. But I've been thinking about Ana-Maria's warning. She said that the curse came when a person looked through the Troll's Eye. Maybe we can go through the doorway without looking."

"We'll ask. But we must go today. Now."

"Just like that?"

"You are a Rover," she whispered, trying for a light tone.

He burst into a big laugh and nodded. "I am a Rover. And, in fact, I already told Ana-Maria we were going."

"What's so funny?"

They whirled to see Master Gimpel coming around the corner of the cathedral.

"Nothing," Laurel said.

Following the mason into the workshop, Laurel went straight to the red stone.

Master Gimpel's eyes lit up. "You want to try the Troll's Eye."

Jassy answered for both of them. "Yes, we want to try it."

"Why now?"

Laurel inhaled sharply. Master Gimpel couldn't say no, not now. "Father is sicker than I thought. Last night– We must go today."

"Ah. You need the white-flowered vine." The mason considered a moment, and then said, "Do you have supplies? Food, travel equipment?"

"Yes," Jassy said.

At Laurel's look of surprise, he shrugged and mouthed, "Rover."

She smiled wryly. He really was a good friend, to anticipate, to be ready.

Jassy swung up his pack and Laurel helped adjust his straps. Over her shoulder, she said, "Another thing: my father will worry when I don't return home tonight."

"Shall I tell him that you went to tend the old man and planned to help Ana-Maria watch through the night?"

Laurel sighed in relief. "Yes. Father will believe that." She went to her corner worktable and uncovered her Christ child carving. "And another thing, if I don't come home, please give this to my father."

Master Gimpel took the carving and turned it around in his hands. Looking up, he said, "You did this?"

She nodded.

"You're talented. When you come back, we'll carve together."

A thrill shot through Laurel. "Thank you, Master." She was almost breathless from the compliment. But she sobered quickly and turned to face the red stone. Laurel was glad that Jassy was an old hand at traveling because she just wanted to run away.

"Ready?"

The mason was too eager, warned Laurel's intuition. But she had no choice. She nodded.

"We've been thinking about the Troll's Eye." Jassy was firm: "We don't want to look through it. We just want to get into the stone world."

Shaking his head, the mason said slowly, as if trying to work out a difficult problem: "But looking through the Troll's Eye is the only way in."

"What if we held hands and just one looked," Laurel insisted. "Would that one pull the other through the Eye?"

"I don't know."

"We'll try it. We need a blindfold so there's no chance of peeking."

Nodding, Jassy dug inside his pack and pulled out a strip of linen."

"Perfect," Laurel took the linen and said, "We'll tie this around your eyes. Turn around."

He nodded, solemn now and turned so Laurel could tie the blindfold.

Laurel hesitated, studying his face, remembering the first time she saw him just a few days ago. His quick action had saved her father, and she only hoped that he would have no reason to save her while they were inside the Troll's Eye. "I'll look through the Troll's Eye," she said firmly. "That means if anything happens to me, you must get us both out."

"I will make sure we are both safe," he promised.

"It's time." The mason lifted his eye patch and pried out the jewel.

Jassy gaped, and Laurel winced, remembering her own surprise. It was time for action, not prayers, but everything within her wanted to run back to the cathedral and stay there.

"Why do you hide it there?" Jassy asked.

"It's one place no one would look for a treasure." The mason held out the gemstone to Laurel.

Quickly, before she could regret it, Laurel put the jewel to her eye and looked through. It was opaque, dark.

Then, the Troll's Eye winked and a door opened, and she could see through the stone.

There was the worktable and the mason–

He was beautiful.

"Wha–" Laurel jerked the jewel away from her eye and thrust it at the mason. "No!"

"What?" Jassy stepped between Laurel and the mason.

Laurel sidestepped him, though, and the feeling of calm from the cathedral overwhelmed her again, and she felt the awe. She reached a finger toward the mason's face, ran the finger gently down his scarred cheek. "Your face was normal," she accused him.

The mason stood still until she dropped her arm to her side.

Jassy looked from one to the other and whispered, "Ugly becomes beautiful. It's the curse. Laurel, this is too dangerous."

Suddenly, she smiled, almost giggled. "It's too easy. And too late now, I've already looked through the Troll's Eye." The stone was warm in her hand. "Besides–" With an effort, she turned away from the mason and concentrated on Jassy. "–everything is the right way now. It was probably nothing."

Master Gimpel said, "The effects of the Troll's Eye build slowly. At first, the reversals come and go. Eventually, though, it changes for good." He took the Troll's Eye from Laurel's hand and fitted it into a hole he had chiseled into the side of the blood-red stone. He interrupted them, "Laurel, look."

Jassy would have stopped her, but she pushed past him and bent to the jewel.

The Troll's Eye winked again, and a door opened. She saw a plateau that stretched fifty feet in front of her until it dropped away to a forested valley below. From somewhere came the sound of tumbling water, and from somewhere overhead, the song of a lark. She wanted to be there, to turn and see the lark, to walk in this strange land.

Jassy tapped her shoulder and she pulled back, reluctant to take her eye away from the sight. As soon as she turned, though, a chill fell on her, and the vision of that other world faded away. She jerked upright and tapped on the stone, suddenly angry. "Where did it go?"

Walking around the stone, she rapped her knuckles, listening for a hollow sound. "Solid. Yet, I saw a world within."

Jassy's eyebrows were knitted in a frown; the mason merely smiled.

"Let's go," Laurel told Jassy.

He held out the linen strip to her. She walked in a mental fog, and it took her a moment to realize what he wanted of her. She tied the linen firmly around his eyes.

As she finished, he grasped her hand. Firm and warm. Steady. She closed her eyes and tried to remember why it was important that Jassy be the steady one. She shook her head; it didn't matter. All that mattered now was to go through the Troll's Eye.

"We're ready," she told the mason.

"Remember, the Eye closes in three days. Only one bag of jewels each can leave the treasure cave, and you must come back out together."

"Yes, yes," Laurel said.

The mason gestured to the jewel still embedded in the stone.

Eager, Laurel bent and stared through the Troll's Eye.

When it winked, the beautiful, strange world lay before her again. She stepped forward, pulling Jassy with her. Strangely, they didn't run into the stone; instead, she grew heavy, and heavier; then she was falling through a deep silence of light and shadow. She stumbled, but Jassy's hand held her. He ripped the linen cloth from his eyes. And together they stood on a mountain plateau.

FIFTEEN

....

L aurel clung to Jassy's hand, an anchor in this new land, and waited for a sudden dizziness to pass.

He grabbed her shoulders and bent to look in her eyes. "What do you see? Did the Troll's Eye hurt you?"

The dizziness had passed, "I'm fine."

Jassy's eyes focused on something behind her.

Whirling, she saw a strange rip in the cliff wall, an opening covered with something like red stained glass. On the other side of this strange window was the workshop they had just left. The old mason was already busy, turning a statue around and around, his head bent to his work. It was the Eye, their way back home. They had to be back here by the end of the third day.

Turning a half circle, Laurel surveyed the land before them. A warm breeze—it was either late spring or early summer here, a few months ahead of their own land—lifted Jassy's curls and blew them around.

"What do you see?" repeated Jassy. "I need to know if we are we seeing the same things."

Her line of sight was blocked by two rows of linden trees with heart-shaped leaves and long branches that formed arches, dividing the plateau into three wide corridors like the nave of a cathedral. The central corridor had deep shadows, with lush splashes of ferns and mosses and occasional yellow flowers. The outer corridors were brilliant in the morning sun, rocky and almost barren.

To their left a waterfall fell about fifteen feet, bounced over monumental boulders, and then tumbled to a stream that flowed toward the edge of the plateau. To the right, the cliff face was a deep red, too steep to climb. The plateau rose slightly from their position, so they couldn't see if a path dropped off of any of the three corridors.

"I see two rows of linden trees and a large plateau," Laurel said.

Jassy let out his breath—Woof! "I do, too. We're in one piece and you're seeing the same thing I do." The corners of his mouth turned up in an attempt at a smile. "We're going to make it."

Laurel was more cautious. "For now, we see the same thing. Master Gimpel said the Troll's Eye affects you slowly."

"But for now—all is well?"

Laurel smiled back, but it was a surface smile. She thought: that must be the way of Rovers, always thinking about the now. But in this stone world, they had to anticipate. She would have to think ahead for both of them.

Jassy turned practical, taking off his cloak in the warm air and stuffing it into his pack. "Which way?"

"You explore one side, I'll take the other."

"No. I'm your shadow for the next three days."

A wave of irritation swept through Laurel. "That's ridiculous. The clock is already ticking. It would be more efficient to have both of us search for the path."

"No. Two in, two out."

"You're right." She took off her cloak, rolled it up and stuffed it into her pack. They had just started, and already she felt heavy, irritable. Breathing deeply to calm herself, she straightened and looked around again. "We still need to find the right path, and I don't see any trail leading anywhere."

A sudden twitching in her apron pocket startled her. Cautious, she reached inside and pulled out her stone gargoyle bird.

It croaked.

She gaped.

The bird raised its head and opened its eyes.

Jassy stood with wide eyes, gawking, and Laurel felt faint.

The bird struggled to stand on its stilt-like legs. Its tiny claws ran across Laurel's palm to her wrist.

Laurel thought: *my bird is alive.*

Then: *It's stone; it can't be alive.*

Then: *I can't enter a stone world either, but here I am.*

She hadn't wanted to gasp, but she knew she had by the way Jassy jerked around to study her, and then jerked back to check on the unnatural bird. Jassy's eyes were huge, bright blue in the bright sun.

"What is it?" he whispered.

Coarse red feathers covered the bird's fat body and scrawny wings. Now, it stretched high and flapped its wings before settling back into Laurel's palm. The tiny claws tightened, digging into her hand. It felt like a bee sting and Laurel flung the bird away.

With a glare back at the Eye, Jassy repeated, "What is it? Something from Master Gimpel?"

"No, no. My father—he gave me the stone bird when I was only five. No—" she paused, confused. "He gave me a stone bird. Why is it alive now?"

The bird flapped across the plateau to the stream to the left, and then hopped onto a boulder and squawked at them. Laurel took a step toward the bird and the squawk turned into a happy chirp. It was like the bird's voice was becoming unfrozen.

Jassy grabbed her arm, "Stop."

She glared at his hand, and then turned her glare to his face.

Dropping his grip, he stepped back and held up both hands in a peace gesture.

In a level voice, she said, "We must follow the bird."

"What?"

"Master Gimpel said we must find the right path. He didn't know we would bring our own guide."

"What makes you think that unnatural creature is a guide?"

"Don't you see? My father said the bird would always protect me. Apparently, here, in the stone world, it is alive. We must trust it."

"I don't like it."

For an answer, Laurel turned and took another step toward the bird, which promptly hopped off its boulder and ran a few steps downstream. Then it stopped and chirped at her.

"Let's follow it," she said.

"No, let's find all the paths we can before we decide."

Without answering, Laurel followed the bird, knowing that Jassy must follow. After all, it was two in, two out.

The bird led past the waterfall to where red rocks and boulders lay jumbled along the stream's edge. When Jassy caught up, his lips were compressed, and his jaw was tight. He was mad.

But Laurel didn't care: she had grown up with her bird and he wouldn't betray her now. It was just logical to follow him.

The stone bird didn't stop: he hopped and flitted over the boulders, leaving Laurel and Jassy to climb up and slide down the jumbled rocks.

It didn't take Jassy long to grumble, "We're going too slowly."

"We could move away from the stream and try to follow."

"No." Jassy hitched up his pack and sighed. "We'd just lose sight of your bird."

Laurel tried to move faster, but the rocks were slick and smooth. In spite of herself, her feet often slipped off into the waters until both boots were soaked. Finally, they came out from behind a large boulder to find the bird waiting for them on a small empty plateau.

Relief flooded through her, "Look!" She pointed along the cliff wall to a well-worn dirt path.

"I hope it's the right path," Jassy said. He slung his pack to the ground and lay down beside the stream to drink. He rolled to his back and said, "We need a short rest."

Laurel drank, too, and then sat up to look around, trying to get her bearings. Their clearing was on the backbone of a great range of mountains. Some peaks were streaked with black or yellow, but most were the blood red of the stone they had entered. Their mountain curved off to the left, forming a U-shaped valley filled with a dense wood.

Jassy pointed across the valley. "If this path is the right one, the treasure cave is in some valley down there."

"It's the right path." Laurel scanned the sides of the mountains, searching for a dark opening. But the mountains curved and folded, hiding their secrets in tucked-away valleys. Now, she shivered. The bird had better be right, or they'd never find the cave.

Suddenly, an urgency filled her, they had no time to sit and daydream.

She hopped up and pulled Jassy up, too. But the sudden energy burst drained her. "It's too hot."

Laurel frowned. Usually her emotions didn't bounce around so wildly. Maybe the mood swings were caused by the Troll's Eye because she couldn't control it.

Jassy grinned, "Be grateful it's not too cold. It's a good day for traveling."

Looking out over the mountain range, the vastness of the world they had entered, she agreed. She was still tired, but her mood swung back to almost giddy, and she leaned her head back and spun around and around. "We made it through the Troll's Eye!"

Joining her laughter, Jassy grabbed her hands and swung her around, and they laughed even more with the joy of being alive and spun around until they collapsed onto the ground, laughing and letting the tension of the last few hours wash away.

"We are alive," Laurel said.

"There's hope for us, yet," Jassy agreed.

Squawk! Awk!

Laurel pointed at her noisy bird. "He says we need to travel."

Jassy nodded and pulled her up. "So now you understand Gargoyle Bird Language?"

Laurel nodded and grinned.

But Jassy sobered. "The bird is right. It's time for speed."

SIXTEEN

....

The rest of the morning's travel was speedy. Laurel had heard travelers speak of a "road coming up to meet you," but now she understood the phrase. The path here was easy and the world was full of joy. Birds flitted and sang sweetly; squirrels scampered along and chattered and scolded them; the streambed sang a lilting melody. Everything was right with their world. Even Laurel's boots were drying out.

As they traveled, Laurel kept watch for the vine with white flowers, but saw nothing. From the description, it should be easy to recognize when they saw it.

By mid-morning, Laurel needed another rest.

Jassy agreed, but warned, "Only a few minutes." He pulled off his pack and lay down in a clump of red clover and closed his eyes.

Even the gargoyle bird rested; perched in a low bush, he turned his head to rest on his back and closed his eyes.

Laurel lay flat along the stream again and drank, and then trailed her hand in the ripples until the cold made her fingers tingle. Sitting up, she spied a white flower. With a beating heart, she shoved aside branches from a bush for a closer look. Maybe it was the white star flower that would heal Father and Antonio. But it was just wild strawberries. She picked a handful and brought them to Jassy.

"Here, lazy. Strawberries." Laurel dropped some on his chest and popped one into her own mouth.

Suddenly, a scalding fire burned all down her throat. "Ahh!" She spit out the berry.

Jassy started up, the berries tumbling into the grass. "What?"

She stuck out her tongue and waved her hand at it.

He picked up a berry from his lap. "You didn't eat this, did you?"

Stumbling up, Laurel staggered to the stream and threw her head into the water and sucked, swishing the cool water around in her mouth, and then spitting it out again. Still it burned. Throwing her head back, she gargled water, and then spat again. Still it burned. She drank and spat again, and yet again, before the fire dimmed to something she could stand. Tears ran down her cheeks and she was sweating.

Jassy knelt beside her, hands by his side, helpless.

"What was it?" she managed to gasp.

"A fire berry."

She stared at the berry in his hand and it wavered, changing shape from a strawberry to a smaller, burgundy fire berry; and then it changed back to a strawberry, so succulent and lovely that she almost wanted to bite it again.

Her voice trembled, "It changes. I can't see it right. Sometimes, it's a fire berry. Sometimes, a strawberry." She sat back on her heels, blinked, and then rubbed her eyes, and when the images kept shifting–fire berry, strawberry, fire berry, strawberry–she clapped her hands over her eyes and wailed, "What's happening to me?"

Jassy's voice was distant, "The Troll's Eye. Bad will be good."

She dropped her hands and stared at him with wide eyes, "I can't trust my vision at all?"

Jassy plucked a flower from the grass. "What's this?"

Laurel hesitated at this test of her vision, but he was right, they had to know. She took the flower and smelled it. She struggled to identify the smell. Laurel felt the shape of the flower, and then smelled it again. "A violet?"

"Yes." Jassy leaned forward and took in a deep breath. "I think you mostly see things right. Before you eat anything else, though, ask me."

Laurel knew he was right, but it aggravated her. She didn't want to depend on him.

Jassy's eyebrows scrunched in concern, but he tried to be encouraging: "We'll be okay. I'm just glad both of us didn't look through the Troll's Eye."

And I'm glad, Laurel thought, *that I didn't come to this world alone.*

For Laurel, the rest of the morning hike passed in a blur. The path still led almost straight down, easy to travel. The bird hopped awkwardly from bush to path to bush again, its long neck bobbing crazily. Yet, Jassy and Laurel were hard pressed to keep up with the clumsy bird's pace. They passed numerous waterfalls where the stream fell toward the valley, but while the path wound up and over small inclines, it was still easy walking. Deep silent pools followed the waterfalls, where sometimes Laurel glimpsed large rainbow-colored fish swimming in the depths. And always, she looked for a vine with white star-shaped flowers.

Once Laurel thought the path jumped, like the rock could move on its own. She was watching her feet on a steep part and suddenly, rubble and debris blocked her way. She closed her eyes and rubbed them quickly.

Opening them again, the path was clear. She wiped her brow, thinking, I'm just tired and hungry.

She almost asked Jassy to stop and rest again but hated to admit her weakness. Instead, she shrugged up her pack and concentrated on watching each step.

Within an hour, they came to a large clearing beside the stream and saw that the path crossed the shallows here and continued on into a wooded area.

"We'll rest here," Jassy said.

Laurel eagerly sat on a rock beside the stream, and stripped off her boots and stockings, and dangled her tiny feet in its cold water. Without speaking, Jassy handed her a piece of bread and cheese and they munched in companionable silence.

After a few bites, Laurel realized her bird was perched on a bush nearby. He was a puzzle she wanted to unravel. At home, she had told the bird many secrets; would he still be a friend in this world?

She pinched off a few crumbs and tossed to him. But he just tilted his impossibly long neck one-way, and then another, chirping merrily, until she laughed.

"Am I making you work too hard?" She threw a crumb closer to the bush. He hopped down and ate it, and then hopped to the first crumb to peck at it.

She threw another, even closer, and then sat still. The bird was motionless, too.

Now she was determined: Father had given her this bird and she wanted him to come to her, to sit on her hand, to comfort her as he had over the years. She threw a breadcrumb right under his beak.

Peck, peck.

He was coming to her.

Hop, peck. Hop, peck. Now the bird was beside her. Moving slowly, she held the bread chunk in her hand and waited.

He hopped onto her leg and started pecking–gently– at the bread. She inched her other hand closer until she could reach out and stroke him, as she had when he was just a stone sculpture; his feathers were soft now and she felt his tiny heartbeat. And suddenly, she wondered how her father was doing: was he coughing again? Had he missed her yet?

But she couldn't think about her father now, or she would lose her courage. She focused on the bird.

Funny, she thought, earlier his feathers were large and coarse. Now they were as soft as goose down.

When the bread was gone, he squawked and flew back to his bush. But it was okay: he would come to her when she needed him.

Leaning back, Laurel lifted hair off her neck and fanned herself. "What will you do with your part of the treasure?"

Jassy's answer was prompt: "Buy a winter house in the south and a large wagon to travel in during the summer months and two white horses to pull it."

Laurel laughed. "You don't need the winter house. You couldn't stay in one place even if you had enough money."

"It's every Rover's dream to have enough money to travel free, to go anywhere and everywhere, but still have a home to come back to."

Laurel suddenly saw him as a noble wanderer, free to come and go at will, free to stay as long as he liked, or to travel as long as he liked. There are worse things in life to want, she thought.

"What will you do with your share?" Jassy asked.

"Buy the quarry, hire the best masons, and build the west tower in only three years instead of a dozen," she answered just as promptly.

Suddenly, Laurel gasped. The sky had turned dark, winds whistled, and the trees were stripped bare of anything green. It was winter.

No. It was almost summer here.

She blinked. And the trees were green, the skies fair and warm.

"What's wrong, Laurel?"

Jassy was holding her hands.

"Things reversed again!"

"What did you see?"

Laurel explained that earlier the path had suddenly been impassable, but that the distortion soon passed. Now, the trees were bare, but changed quickly back to green. "What is real in this crazy place?"

Jassy's mouth tightened. "I'm worried. The deeper we go into this world, the more the Troll's Eye is affecting you."

It was true. But there was nothing they could do except move on. With great effort, Laurel forced a smile. She reached for her stockings and boots and when she did, the gargoyle bird woke and flapped off to a nearby bush. She dried her feet with her skirt and tugged on her boots. Looking up, Jassy's brow was still furrowed. "I'm fine," she said.

"You're not fine." But he offered her a hand up anyway and insisted: "When you see strange things, you must tell me. Every time."

"I will." The words were easy, but Laurel knew she wouldn't—couldn't worry Jassy with her problem.

The words satisfied Jassy, though. He shifted his pack, readjusting its weight, and then waved at the red bird, which flew across the stream. Rocks and boulders lay exposed in the shallow stream. Jassy jumped lithely from rock to rock. Laurel picked up her pack and staff, and then turned to look back up the mountain. She studied the faint red glimmer from the Troll's Eye.

When she turned back, Jassy was just disappearing around a bend and a whistled melody floated back to her. Was it the whistle of the wind in bare winter trees, or Jassy whistling?

She glanced back up the cliff and heard again Master Gimpel's words: "Two in, two out."

Aloud, she said, "Treasure. For my father. For the cathedral."

And Laurel gritted her teeth against the winter wind, shouldered her pack and followed the bird and the boy.

SEVENTEEN

J assy and the red bird set a smooth, steady pace. Their way rose and fell and twisted through woods. Under the tree canopy, it was cool and dim; pine needles underfoot sent up sharp incense. Laurel managed to keep her vision steady, but it wearied her. Muscles, unused to so much hiking, ached as well.

Suddenly Jassy stopped ahead. Looking over his shoulder, Laurel saw that the path split.

Jassy raised an eyebrow. "Which way?'

To Laurel, they were both just dim corridors.

"Look," Jassy said, "the bird is taking the left path."

Laurel's vision suddenly shifted. Something wild, a beast, blinked at her from beyond the bird. It was leading them straight into the beast's path. "Right, Jassy, go right." Fearful, she tugged at his sleeve.

Jassy narrowed his eyes. "What's wrong? Your eyes again?"

She stared at him, fear mounting with each passing second. She couldn't trust him; he didn't see what she saw; he didn't understand the dangers.

"No," she lied. Wicked yellow beast-eyes followed her every movement. "Just don't trust–" She stopped, uncertain. "–don't trust that bird."

"But it's your bird, your guardian. Close your eyes, Laurel! Now! Something is very wrong."

The beast crept forward on its belly, straight for Laurel's feet. She couldn't trust Jassy; he wanted her to close her eyes, wanted the beast to attack. It wasn't large, but when it opened its mouth, sharp rows of teeth gleamed at her.

She turned, slapping away Jassy's hands, and fled down the right-hand path, shoving aside branches, trampling bushes and racing, hearing the breathing of the beast right behind her, knowing that at any moment, it would leap at her.

Jassy was yelling, but she couldn't stop to listen to that traitor.

She ran flat out, charging ahead.

The path led up a hill and she gasped, struggling for air, struggling to run full speed, to escape the beast.

Jassy was closer now: "Stop! Slow down!"

She did slow down, but not because she wanted to. She wheezed, trying to catch her breath. But she forced one foot to go in front of the other. She topped the hill and stood, teetering on the edge of a hole.

The ground dropped away twenty feet into the ground where a dark abyss disappeared into nothing. Twenty feet across, the edge of the bowl-shaped hole was overgrown with small shrubs and grasses. Laurel cried out in fear. She waved her arms wildly, trying to stop her forward movement. Then, her foot slipped and she fell—

–almost fell. Instead, Jassy grabbed at her, catching hold of her dress, pulling, and catching her arm, her waist and pulling her away from the hole, pulling her backwards until they tumbled together down the same hill they had just climbed. They crashed into a large shrub.

After a stunned moment, Jassy rolled to his knees and turned her over. His hands desperately shoved hair and leaves away from her face, "Laurel!"

She groaned and blinked up at him. "What happened?"

Struggling, she managed to sit up. She plucked a leaf from her hand and held it out to stare at it.

"Are you all right?" Jassy's brows were knitted in concern, and his voice was high, strained.

She held out the leaf to Jassy and gave a slight shake of her head.

He sighed. "You almost ran into a sink hole. There must be caves all over these hills. Sometimes a natural opening to a cave is a hole just like that one. And it's hidden until you get right on top of it."

Laurel's hand trembled, and she dropped the leaf. "You saved my life."

"Why did you run?"

"There was a wild beast. The bird. He was leading us straight toward some wild thing."

"Are you talking about the squirrel?"

A squirrel. Laurel buried her face in her hands, scared to open her eyes, scared of what she might—or might not—see. "What are we going to do?"

"You must trust me."

"I want to."

"I almost didn't catch you."

"The curse–" She stopped and looked up at him, at his wide eyes, at the leaves that clung to his hair, at his shaking hand. "I didn't trust you. I wanted to, but the curse–"

He held up his hands in frustration. "You must try."

"Yes. I'll try," she said. But they both understood now that she might not be able to trust him. Yet, what could they do? They had to continue on.

Laurel stood up and leaned unsteadily on a small sapling. After a moment, they turned downhill and went back to the split in the path. Though they hunted, the red bird was gone.

"He could be anywhere by now," Jassy said.

Laurel didn't want to leave the gargoyle bird behind; he was their only guide in this cold, stone world. And she didn't want him left alone in this world, either.

Now, she had only Jassy to travel with.

And come to think of it, why should she trust Jassy? She knew so little about him, really had only known him a few days. And besides, who can trust a Rover? Everyone had warned her against him, maybe they were right.

No, that was the curse talking. She could trust Jassy. Must trust him. There was no choice but to forge onward.

"I just hope we don't have any more forks in the path," she said.

They marched for another hour without incident until the trees thinned and the sun sank to become a fiery ball sitting on the dark cliffs.

Now the woods stopped abruptly, giving way to an alpine meadow with outcroppings of red rock set in the midst of yellow flowers. Long shadows from the cliff crept across the meadow almost to their feet.

"At last!" Laurel hadn't realized how the dark woods had worn away at her. She sank onto a flat red stone covered with grey lichens. Suddenly, she leaned forward and picked the leaf of a plant that grew beside the stone and rolled it in her fingers to be sure it had square stems. "Mint! Do we have time for a fire and a cup of tea?"

Jassy dropped his pack beside her. "No. But we both need it."

He went back and forth to the woods, bringing firewood while Laurel picked a couple handfuls of mint. When the wood was ready, he took a tinderbox from his pack and soon had a merry fire burning. He poured water from his flask into a tiny pot and set it over two red stones at the fire's edge. Then he stretched out on the rock beside her. "We've made good time."

This was a good time to find out more about him, Laurel decided. "How long have you been on the road?"

"Five summers."

"Antonio isn't your father. Why do you travel with him?"

"He's my mother's brother. He had no children until he took in Ana-Maria when she was orphaned. It's hard to travel, though, with just one child for help. We have eight children—a large family with many mouths to feed. When Antonio asked me to travel with him, I was glad to go, to see new places."

"All I've seen are rock quarries," she sighed. "Lots of them. But somehow, I don't like traveling far from the cathedral. It's my home."

Jassy shook his head, "I am more comfortable traveling than staying at home."

So strange to wander so far from home, Laurel thought. And to enjoy it. Although, in an odd way, she supposed, she was still inside the red stone, inside Master Gimpel's workshop, inside the cathedral. The water was boiling now, so she dropped in mint leaves and let them steep, and then poured tea into tin mugs for each of them.

"You remind me of my youngest sister," Jassy said. "She knows herbs, too."

"Tell me about her."

Jassy shrugged. "She's eight and already as tall as you. And she loves to tease."

"What does she tease you about?" Laurel closed her eyes and sipped her tea, enjoying the familiar warmth.

"Loyalty."

She raised an eyebrow.

"I'm very loyal," he protested. "Once I decide to commit to something or someone, I will never waver."

But just then, he did waver; he was a short, squat gargoyle who was drinking tea. No, it was just Jassy, with his curly hair, his serious blue eyes.

No. He was a gargoyle with shiny eyes. "I never waver," repeated the gargoyle.

Laurel stared at Jassy's pointy ears and wanted to cry. It was bad enough when the landscape shifted, and squirrels became monsters. But for Jassy to change, it was almost unbearable.

Was this trip worth the misery? She swirled the tea in her cup. "Will we find the treasure?"

Jassy stretched and then set down his tea mug. "You stay here and rest. I'll scout around."

"No!" A fear gripped her, fear that the entire world would shift again while he was out of sight. "No, two in and two out. We stay together."

"You're right."

She flinched when his gargoyle-like claws reached for her, grasped her and pulled her up. But then his hands—not his claws—turned her loose.

Trying to stay calm, Laurel brushed twigs and grasses from her yellow skirt, and then turned toward the cliff. Dusk was rapidly approaching. "The path peters out here, but it was heading that way," she said. "We could head straight across the meadow. Also, I've been forgetting to watch for the white-flowered vine."

"I've been watching but haven't seen anything yet."

The meadow was in a valley, and they had decided to follow the cliff, but which direction? Right or left?

"We'll try one direction for ten minutes, and then backtrack and try the other direction," said Jassy-the-human-boy.

"Shhh!"

"What?"

"Shhh!" Laurel nodded toward a clump of wild rosemary that shook slightly. "Just barely saw something. Went in there."

Jassy waved at her to go around the left of the bush, while he went around the right.

Again, the rosemary rustled. Maybe it was just another squirrel. But Laurel hoped it was the red bird, come back to help them.

Without warning, Jassy lunged toward the rosemary bushes yelling.

She yelled, too, but stood still, content to let Jassy, chase whatever it was.

Then, Jassy turned and ran toward the trees, calling over his shoulder. "Laurel! Run!"

She fled with him toward the tree line, but suddenly stopped. She was overcome with a sweet odor, like a flower garden or a scented herb garden on a sunny day; no, even better, like the cinnamon the merchants had brought to market last year. "Jassy! What's happening?"

Jassy turned and saw that she had stopped. He stumbled back toward her, coughing and gagging. "Oh! The smell!" He rubbed his nose vigorously and waved his hand. His face was twisted in a look of agony.

"The flowers, the cinnamon?" Confusion swept over her. "Jassy?"

"You don't smell the skunk?"

Laurel could do nothing but stare. Then, she sniggered. No, she couldn't stop it, great belly laughs poured out of her until she had to sit, gasping for air, yet still giggling. "The Troll's Eye," she gasped. "Bad will be good. Skunks smell like cinnamon."

Jassy-the-human-boy didn't smile back, but just held his nose and rolled his eyes. "Well, it smells awful to me. Let's go."

And just as suddenly, Laurel sobered. And hiccupped. If she couldn't see right or smell right, could she trust herself at all? And there was still the question of whether or not she could trust Jassy. He said loyalty was his only flaw. But that said nothing about whether he told the truth or not, nothing about whether she could trust him. Where was her bedrock? Because she had to trust–

She rubbed her eyes. It couldn't be, not here. There, across the valley, a dark stream of color drifted higher and higher. It looked like–. But it couldn't be–.

She pointed, "Look! Smoke!"

EIGHTEEN

A bout a quarter mile away, a black column of smoke streamed lazily upward, curling around the heights of the cliff.

Jassy grabbed Laurel's hand in excitement. "It's not smoke; it's bats."

"The cave!" Laurel tilted her head up to watch the dark stream. "There must be thousands of them."

The first of the bats reached high into the dark sky, and then spread out and disappeared like smoke dissipating in the wind; but the column continued unabated as more bats poured out of the cave.

Jassy said, "We'll wait an hour and make sure the Hallvard is asleep. Then, we'll enter the cave."

Laurel agreed, and they returned to their campfire. The skies deepened into an eerie black where no stars twinkled. Instead, far across the valley, they saw the only moon in this strange world: a dim red glow that marked the Troll's Eye doorway back to their own world.

Opening his pack, Jassy pulled out linen strips and a crock of black pitch. "We need to make torches."

"You really did come prepared." Laurel helped dip linen strips into the pitch and then wrap them around sturdy sticks. The smell was putrid, or at least she thought it was. "Jassy, what if my vision gets worse? The cave will be dangerous."

"Do we have a choice?" Flickering firelight played across Jassy's grim face.

She was glad that, for now, he looked like himself, like a normal boy. "I'm scared."

He nodded. "But we can do it. Together, we'll make it." He jabbed the torches upright in the dirt, waiting till they headed to the cave.

Laurel tried to wipe the sticky pitch off her fingers by rubbing them in a clump of grass. Would the cave really be full of jewels? She jumped up and paced before the fire, flicking her yellow skirt with each turn back in the other direction.

She glanced up to see if the stars had moved, but of course, there were no stars. Only that red doorway far up on the cliff. She rubbed her eyes, but that made her even jumpier. And her fingers still stank of pitch. Ironically, she wished the curse would change it to some good smell.

Too much waiting! "Jassy, let's go!"

He yawned but agreed. "You're right. We'll leave our packs here. Just take your torch."

Jassy added two more large branches to the fire to keep it going while they were gone. Then he thrust his torch into the flames and Laurel lit her torch, as well.

They walked side by side across the meadow to the dark bulk of the cliff, and then turned left along the cliff face. Shadows jumped and shifted in the torchlight.

Laurel grimaced but managed to hold on to a true vision—she hoped. The wind picked up and moaned softly through the dark spiky firs behind them. Clouds scudded darkly across the sky. Or was it all her imagination?

Jassy stopped and pointed ahead.

Before them gaped a ragged arch-like hole with mosses dripping from the edges. Laurel wrinkled her nose at the damp, musty smell and wished that this smell would reverse, too. She shifted her torch to the other side and tucked her free hand into Jassy's. The torch sizzled, whispering something unintelligible to her, perhaps a final warning.

Jassy squeezed her hand in reassurance, and then pulled her forward. Breathing too fast, her stomach clenched with fear, Laurel clung to Jassy's hand as if it was a lifeline.

A single tunnel led deep into the ground, the warm air growing cooler, damper. Even the darkness changed from an open sky to a dark so thick their torches barely pierced it. They crept along the somber passage, trembling.

"How far?" Laurel's voice—the merest whisper—echoed, and she cringed.

Jassy shook his head and Laurel nodded agreement. Until they found the treasure chamber and knew more about the Hallvard, they had to be cautious.

Laurel concentrated on listening for something besides themselves. She tilted her head back and forth and tried to penetrate the darkness outside their pool of light.

Was the Gargoyle Man right; was it safe to enter the cave at night?

What was that?

Laurel spun around, but there were only their own eerie shadows floating on the cave wall. She rested one hand on the corridor wall, needing something solid to reassure her. It was wet. And cold. Not like Jassy's warm hand which still held hers. Cold and warm, a strange reality. But the contrast helped ground her, kept her from yelling out, from worrying that the curse was taking over again.

There were only the small sounds of water dripping and their muted footsteps. No, their steps were too loud, the chink of pebbles against stone. A cold fear spread through her, but fear of what, she didn't know, just that she was shivering. Now, her breathing came in ragged gasps.

Something flew straight at her face.

Laurel screamed. She dropped her torch and jerked her hand away from Jassy to cover her face. Desperate, she dropped to her knees away from whatever it was.

Instantly, Jassy was there, helping her up. "Only a bat," he murmured. But he looked over his shoulder where they had come from and then looked forward, studying the corridor.

Laurel realized that if anyone or anything was ahead, her scream had alerted them that she and Jassy were coming. "Sorry," she snapped. "It scared me." She fumed at herself for getting spooked.

Grumpily, she straightened her blouse and skirt and picked up her torch, which was still lit.

Jassy soothed, "It's your first time in a cave."

She nodded. She'd been in Jassy's cave, of course, but had never gone out of sight of the entrance.

"Pretend it's a quarry with a lid on it. You aren't scared in a quarry."

That description did make the cave sound friendlier. "I'll try," Laurel said.

They walked on for five minutes until the corridor opened into a small chamber, maybe twenty arm-spans long and ten arm-spans wide.

Jassy waved his torch, lighting up the dark places, "Two exits. Now what?"

"We need the red bird." The tiny moment of calm was gone as she wondered if they'd ever see the stone bird again. And would he really have known which corridor to take? She fumed at herself for losing him so quickly, the only chance they had of a navigator in this land.

Jassy left her standing in the middle of the room and poked his head into each opening and smelled. He turned back and shrugged, "Which way?"

Grimacing, Laurel said, "Left. Last time the left fork was correct."

"As good a guess as any."

They ducked through the low doorway into the passage and found that it plunged deeper into the rock. Again, they held hands, helping each other balance. But the passage quickly narrowed, forcing them to go single file. Jassy led, his hissing torch creating a dim pool of light that overlapped the gleam from Laurel's torch. The steep slope jammed Laurel's toes into the end of her boot and made her calves ache.

Eventually, the passage leveled and opened up. Then it dropped off five feet to a lower level.

"I'll go first," Jassy said. He handed his torch to Laurel, turned and edged over the drop-off, landing on his feet. Carefully, Laurel dropped down Jassy's torch and he caught it. But she didn't notice him stoop to set down the torch until she was already dropping hers. It fell in the dirt and before he could catch it back up, the cloud of dust extinguished the flames.

"Don't worry, I'll relight it after you get down," Jassy said. He picked up his torch again and held it high for Laurel to see better.

Behind him, Laurel saw a great chasm that stretched away into darkness.

In the dim light, she saw a bridge, a stone arch over the chasm, something they could easily cross over.

Jassy had said nothing about a chasm or a bridge; they must be illusions. She gritted her teeth, turned and grabbed the edge of the rock and dropped her legs over the edge. She searched for a toehold, but finally had to just drop. She landed with a thud and sat abruptly.

Jassy leaned over. "Are you–"

His hand had coarse black hair and claws!

Laurel sprang up, and as she did, her head knocked Jassy's arm. Jassy's torch flew away and they spun around to watch it fall and fall and fall and fall, until it was just a bright spark, and still it fell until, finally, it disappeared.

Inky blackness engulfed them.

Laurel fell to her knees and clutched a handful of dirt in frustration. The chasm was real! And deep.

"Jassy!" She panicked–

"Here." He touched her head.

"Oh, I was afraid you–" With effort, she drew deep breaths and calmed herself. "What now?"

"Your torch. We'll find it and relight it with my flint box."

"I'm not moving." The dark was too complete to even think about moving.

"Fine, I will lie down and stretch out and feel around for your torch. You just hold my feet, so I don't lose you in the dark."

"Hurry."

Laurel shivered, her fear growing: fear of the dark, fear of the Hallvard, fear of the Troll's Eye curse. They had to hurry. Or she wouldn't make it. She held onto Jassy's boots while he stretched flat out and groped around for her torch.

"Can't find it." Jassy's voice was strained, too.

Laurel bit her lip. She didn't want Jassy to move away from her touch. "I'll scoot along the wall we just came down. Then you can try again."

Still shivering, she pushed her back against the rough wall and slid right about two feet and held onto his boots. Again, Jassy stretched forward, patting about, searching for the torch and raising dust.

Laurel sneezed. Miserable, she closed her eyes and opened them—no difference, just black, a void. She took one hand away from his boot and jammed that fist into her eye until stars swam before her, a welcome sight. But the stars weren't real. She wondered: How many years did it take a skeleton to turn to dust?

"Go right a couple more feet."

Laurel obeyed, and Jassy stretched away from her, patting the dirt.

She leaned her head back against the wall and clenched her teeth. "Hurry."

"I found it!"

Laurel exhaled in relief. Funny how dark was darker without the torch. Even unlit, the torch—the possibility of light—made the dark easier to bear.

Jassy crawled back to Laurel and handed her the torch. He fumbled with his pack until he found his flint box and struck a couple sparks. Finally, a circle of light surrounded them again, chasing away the suffocating darkness.

Cautiously, they crawled to the edge of the drop off. Laurel's heart pounded in her ears. "It doesn't have a bottom. Or a bridge."

The chasm was fifty arm-spans across and the bottom was lost beyond the reach of their torchlight. Jassy held up the torch and dropped a rock; they listened for it to hit bottom. Nothing.

"I saw a bridge over this hole. What happened to it? And why didn't you see this?"

"I was concentrating on getting down. And you really saw a bridge?"

"Now I'm seeing things that aren't there. What next?"

"Blast it! I don't know." Then, softer, "I don't know."

"–don't know–" echoed the cave.

This time, Laurel threw a fistful of dirt into the chasm. She wanted to scream and rage, hit and cry.

"I don't know," Jassy repeated and gently touched her shoulder.

Turning, there he was, and he folded her in a one-armed embrace. He was a warm body in this cold place, and it comforted her to have another human with her.

Quickly, though, Jassy moved away. "We've lost time."

"Yes." Laurel rose and went back to the five-foot wall and climbed. Jassy handed up the torch, and then climbed up himself. They trudged back up the steep passage to the small chamber and into the right-hand passage.

It was a level and straight corridor this time, widening steadily as they plodded along.

Laurel needed reassurance. "Jassy, we will build the cathedral tower, won't we?"

"We'll build."

"And Father will live to see it built?"

"He will."

Jassy's promise was enough, for now, Laurel thought.

The roof rose steadily above them now, until it was lost outside the reach of torchlight. They walked as if through the arched corridors of the cathedral, as if this was tutored stone, elegant in its design, organized and deepened by the endless ages of water that carved mountains from the inside out.

The corridor curved gradually and opened into a large chamber that extended off into the dark.

Jassy held up his torch and whistled in wonder. "The treasure room!"

Before them lay heaps of stones: flashing rubies, rich emeralds, brilliant diamonds, and lustrous opals. They weren't strewn haphazardly, rather were arranged neatly upon stone shelves along the wall. Not in strict order, but with a casualness that gave the room an opulent feel, a room meant for royalty.

Laurel stepped forward to see better.

Suddenly, she felt eyes watching her. She whirled to the right. Over her loomed a huge bear with its long yellow claws outstretched.

She screamed.

NINETEEN

....

J assy shoved Laurel away from the creature, dove under the sharp claws and rolled away. Laurel lay where she fell with eyes squeezed shut, expecting claws to dig into her.

But nothing happened.

After a moment, she opened her eyes. The first thing she saw was Jassy crouched and staring at the creature. She was glad to see that he was still holding the torch.

Ignoring her, Jassy stood and circled the stone figure that guarded the chamber's entrance. "It's sleeping," he said when he was sure.

Laurel's cheeks flushed. "Sleeping," she said in disgust. It was embarrassing to be so scared of something frozen in stone. She tried to ignore the creature and look around. She dusted her skirts, sighed and let curiosity pull her to Jassy's side, where they both stared at the Hallvard. He was bear-like, but too massive to be a real bear. Over ten feet tall, the sculpture was perfect in every detail, even the individual hairs on his pelt were perfectly done.

"He looks so real," she whispered. Then wondered why she had whispered, since stone sculptures couldn't hear.

"He is real," Jassy said. "He just can't move at night, remember?"

This close, she heard the creature breathing: in, out, in, out. And his hateful yellow eyes followed her movements, she was sure of it.

She darted back to Jassy and hid behind him. "He's looking at me."

Startled, Jassy turned and stared at her face. "What do you mean?"

The Hallvard's yellow eyes must be some kind of strange jewel, she thought.

When she didn't answer, Jassy said, "He can't move till dawn. Let's fill our bags and leave." He waved at a large brass scale near the door. Beside it was a jumbled stack of bags. It took Jassy a few minutes to sort out the sacks and choose the smallest of the brass weights, the one Master Gimpel had called a Troll's Weight. "Here." Jassy handed Laurel a small canvas sack. "Fill this with whatever jewels you want and then we'll weigh it."

Laurel turned to look at the jewels but blinked. The mounds of jewels were only heaps of pebbles and rubbish. She stumbled forward, uncertain, "Where did the jewels go?"

Jassy was already holding several brown pebbles. Without looking up, he snapped, "What now?"

She watched him pick up several more pebbles, roll them around, heft them, smell them, taste them.

Then, he looked up with a look of pure joy. "Look at all this! Such treasure!"

Disgusted, Laurel tossed him her bag. "Here, fill mine, too."

"Really? OK."

It wasn't fair, she thought crossly. He's having all the fun and all I get are pebbles.

Something tugged at the edge of her vision. There. By the wall.

What was it?

Laurel tiptoed around heaps of rubble toward the far wall. Jassy was so involved in his worthless jewels that he wouldn't notice if she wandered around.

Something along the wall gleamed red. She bent and picked it up. A ruby! She caressed the oval stone and admired how it fit so comfortably in her small hand, as if it had been made just for her. It was her gemstone, her ruby.

She put it to her eye and the familiar winking door opened. It was a Troll's Eye.

Turning slowly, she studied the treasure chamber through the lens of the Troll's Eye: it was full of jewels. Glittering. Enticing.

She took the Troll's Eye away from her eyes. Just worthless pebbles again.

Oh, what was happening to her? What was real? She thought it was a good sign that she could still ask this question. But that didn't help her know what was real and what was an illusion. She couldn't trust her senses any longer. There was a reality, something was there, but her ability to see and hear and touch and smell that reality was gone; the curse of the Troll's Eye was real. Instead, she had to believe that the reality was there despite herself. And how long could she believe in what she couldn't see? Laurel closed her fist tightly over the ruby jewel.

Suddenly, the cave rumbled ominously. Startled, Laurel turned back to the cave wall, but it was moving, slipping. A great jumble of loose rocks, stones and boulders stretched away toward the ceiling somewhere above–she had forgotten how high the ceiling was–and those rocks were sliding toward her.

"Laurel! Look out!"

She was looking, she thought dumbly. A layer of rocks peeled off and plummeted toward her. Her feet moved, trying to run, but the rockslide tripped her. She fell, banging her right hip. Around her, stones rumbled, and rock dust billowed.

Somehow, she held on to her jewel; the Hallvard would not make her turn loose of it, for she was sure that this was his doing somehow. He knew what was valuable here, just like she did. Jassy was the fool, grabbing at those pebbles.

"Laurel! Where are you?"

She coughed and breathed deeply. But rock dust filled her lungs, not air. She coughed again, struggling, gasping, suddenly desperate for air. Then, she actually got a breath. The rock dust was already subsiding, and she could barely see that the rockslide–at least most of it–had fallen on her left-hand side.

"Here."

Jassy was beside her instantly, jerking her up and away from the rubble. "What are you doing?" He glared, yelled, "When I saw that rock sliding–" Suddenly, he sat down hard, put his head between his knees and breathed hard and fast until he could look up with a chalk-white face and say, "I thought you were gone."

"And you were worried you would never get out of this stone world." With her hand, she fanned at the rock dust. Flippant—a response to her fear a moment earlier—she said, "Don't worry, nothing can kill me. I'll live forever."

Then, looking around, she realized that she wasn't okay; something had changed. Before the rockslide, the jewels had looked like pebbles, and that had been wrong. They still looked the same, they were just pebbles, but it didn't bother her any longer. It was like the world had been flip-flopping around, and it had finally straightened up. That it was upside down didn't matter, as long as it was going to stay this way. The curse had completely taken hold, and everything was reversed.

....

TWENTY

"**I** am fine," she told him. Jassy didn't need to know. She checked her legs, running a hand up and down each leg, transferring the jewel from right to left hand as she did it. Her yellow skirt was ripped on the left side, her right leg was bruised, but miraculously, nothing was broken. "I'm fine."

"Then, sit. Right there," Jassy said.

Why was his voice so cheerful? She realized, that in her new reality, it meant he was angry. "Don't move while I finish weighing the bags," he ordered. "Then, we'll leave."

Laurel sat, suddenly tired and content to do nothing.

Jassy picked his way through the rubble back to where his torch was stuck upright in a pile of black stones beside the Troll's scale. He picked up one canvas bag and set it on the scale. It tipped toward the bag—it was too heavy—so Jassy took out one stone. Reluctantly, he hefted it in his hand, and then tossed it aside. The scale balanced now, and he tied it shut and quickly repeated the process with the other bag.

Laurel put her hand right beside her skirt and hid it from Jassy's view. Then she opened her fist: the Troll's Eye twinkled brightly and she smiled. Not even a rockslide could take it away from her, she thought smugly. Let Jassy take both those bags of ugly rocks, she had the one true treasure. She closed her fist and jammed it into her pocket.

With her free hand, Laurel pushed herself up and took a tentative step. Nothing hurt, so she took another step and finally climbed over and through the rocks toward Jassy.

"Ready?" she called.

He held out the bag. "Did you find any jewels to add to your bag?"

"No."

"Too bad we can only take two bags." Jassy looked ruefully around the chamber. "Do you think we could ever come back for more?"

For this pile of junk? Laurel rolled her eyes.

"You're right, it's too dangerous."

Laurel picked up the torch and let Jassy carry both bags. As she sidled past the bear-like Hallvard, she felt his eyes on her again. She forced herself to turn loose of the Troll's Eye in her pocket and to grip the torch with both hands.

The Hallvard's yellow eyes bored into her.

No! The bags of jewels were for the cathedral and her father. But the Troll's Eye was hers. She glared back at the Hallvard and whispered, "It's mine."

Suddenly the cave was filled with the Hallvard's growl, a melodious sound to Laurel. But she knew enough to be scared: He was solid stone, yet he growled.

Laurel turned and fled. Through the long corridors, she raced. She vaguely knew that Jassy was following, but even if he wasn't, she wouldn't slow down. They had to get back to the Troll's Eye doorway as fast as possible.

Laurel pounded toward the cave entrance, ready to dash out toward their fire in the meadow. But she stopped short at the sight of water cascading across the cave's entrance. It fell in sheets from the mosses around the opening. She leaned over, trying to catch her breath and heard Jassy thud up beside her.

A streak of lightning lit up the meadow, followed by a clap of thunder.

Jassy waved a hand at the scene. "The sky was almost clear when we came in."

"What can we do?"

From the depths came another deep growl.

She flinched.

"Laurel, what did you say to the Hallvard?"

"Nothing." Her voice was tight.

"He's not supposed to be angry. We each took one bag of jewels each. I weighed them, and they are only a Troll's Weight each. We followed the rules."

"And where'd we get those rules? You think that Master Gimpel told us everything? We were fools to trust him."

Jassy's eyes narrowed, "We have to trust him. And he warned us, once we step outside this cave, we can't return any jewels." He handed Laurel one bag of jewels. "If you have anything else, put it in the bag now."

She shook her head; she would not let him see her Troll's Eye.

Jassy's mouth was tight. "Okay. We have no choice. Rain or not, dark or not, we must go because the Troll's Eye closes in two days. Leave the torch, it's worthless. I have more linen and pitch in my pack if we need it later." He held out his hand.

Laurel sighed, suddenly weary at the sight of his gargoyle's claw, but took it anyway. Clutching her Troll's Eye in her other hand, she let Jassy pull her through the watery doorway and out of the cave.

Laurel and Jassy exited the treasure cave and immediately a warm rain hit her face, a gentle wind tugged at her clothes. Her hair was instantly soaked, dripping, but the water running over her face, down her neck was pleasant.

But Jassy tugged at her and, as they ran, she realized the curse was making everything backwards. The wind was probably cold—yes, she was shivering. And Jassy's clothes were billowing behind him; the wind was probably whipping about. It was scarier than if she felt the wind and cold rain.

Running, Jassy kept one hand on the cliff to keep his bearings.

Laurel strained against the darkness. "Is that our fire? Over there." She turned Jassy around to see and had to guide his face with her hand until he was looking the right direction.

Jassy nodded and pulled her along toward the fire. But even as they ran, the fire dwindled. Laurel longed for the mason's workshop and her father's deep voice rumbling on about the cathedral. She wanted to show her Christ child to Master Benoit and the other stone masons and carvers, to show them that she had worked hard all winter while they were back home with their families.

Instead, their campfire was only dim embers when they reached it, and even those coals were sputtering in the rain. Hurriedly, they gathered their utensils and re-packed. Laurel pulled out her cloak and threw it over her shoulders. For a moment, it was cold, uncomfortable; but the rain soon soaked it, making it light and warm. Yet she stood miserable, shivering.

It wasn't often she was ashamed of what she did. She spent lonely hours in the woods searching for herbs, dried them, and readied them for tending the sick. When townsmen called on her, she offered what she could to those with fevers, boils, broken bones or aching teeth. Even in this quest, she had come for her father. And for her love of the cathedral. And yes, for selfish reasons, too. She wanted to be a stone carver. She didn't want to leave the only home she had ever known.

But she hadn't come for the love of money. Never!

Yet, the whole trip felt dingy, now, like she had planned to steal. No! She hadn't planned anything. But, the heavy bag pleased her, the knowledge of the jewels it contained pleased her. And her Troll's Eye in her pocket absolutely delighted her. She was ashamed.

She bowed her head and held her hands out to the warm rain, hoping it would cleanse her. Jassy was watching and she stepped away from his gaze, out of the firelight. The grasses were slick, though, and she tripped and fell into a muddy puddle.

Jassy held out a gargoyle hand—he always looked deformed to her now.

She hesitated, not wanting to get him dirty, too.

But he grabbed her and heaved her up. "Let's get to the trees and make a shelter under some bushes."

"No!" Laurel exploded. "I want to get out of here. We need to run all the way back. Now."

Jassy soothed, "We'll be fine, we have two days to get back. And I'm too tired to go much farther on such a dark and stormy night."

Laurel wanted desperately to get the mud off her cloak, her clothes, herself. She pulled her hands away and wiped them on her skirt, leaving a dark streak of mud— which looked beautiful, even in the dim firelight. Which aggravated her even more. She grunted in frustration and Jassy turned to look at her.

"I'm worried," Laurel said. "The Gargoyle Man told me that when he does a sculpture, he just lets out what he sees in the rock. His gargoyles are so realistic. What if he tries to trap people in his rocks, so he can carve them?"

"That's crazy!" Jassy just shook his head and turned toward the tree line.

*   *   *

Water dripped from leaves, twigs, and grass blades. It ran into tiny rivulets that joined larger trickles that rushed into streams that hadn't been there the day before. Dozens of streams, which had been re-born in the night's storm, now tumbled toward the only river that ran through the valley. As dawn broke, water was on the move everywhere, rushing to join a stream: tumbling, gurgling, sweeping away everything that stood in its path in the mad jubilant march to join the river.

And with the dawning, the Hallvard came.

The first rays of light released him from his nocturnal stone. He growled softly and shambled up the corridor of the treasure cave. The rain had washed away any scent or tracks of the thieves, but he didn't need them anyway. The tiny thief had taken an extra jewel, which would draw him like a lodestone.

The great beast came out into the wet, washed meadow. He stood on his hind legs and looked around, as if getting his bearings. He raised his muzzle to the sky and roared once. And then, again. He dropped to all fours and loped across the meadow and into the woods beyond. He would not rest until he had all the jewels safely back in the cave.

*   *   *

Laurel yawned and stretched. Then she jerked straight upright. It was almost dawn; the sky was starting to lighten.

Nearby, Jassy yawned and asked sleepily, "What?"

"It's morning. That's all."

Standing up, every muscle ached. She refused to look at her hands and clothes: she knew they were dirty but was afraid that if she looked she would see a bright yellow tunic and skirt with a spotless black cape.

Jassy was sitting up now, untying the string of his jewel sack. He blinked sleepily at her. "Did we dream all that last night?" He shook a few stones into his hand and Laurel stopped to watch.

Jassy's hand held only pebbles.

Laurel's hand brushed her skirt pocket. Ah, yes, her stone, the only real jewel. She smiled to herself.

Jassy stood now and stretched. "You look mean and scruffy today," he said good-naturedly. "There's mud on your face and your hair is a mess. Let's get cleaned up and on the road."

Laurel nodded agreement, already anxious to get going. Taking a comb from her pack, she went toward the noisy clanging of a nearby stream. She splashed water on her face, feeling her eyes, cheekbones and forehead. She sighed in relief to feel only her own skin and familiar curves. She and Jassy were both here in the stone world, together, and it didn't matter that she alone had looked through the Troll's Eye. They would make it out together. She shook water from her face and repeated to herself: Two in, two out.

Glancing back to be sure Jassy wasn't close, she pulled out her stone and swished it in the water, washing it. Then she held it up to admire its glitter. The first rays of dawn filtered through the trees to be caught up in the stone and make it gleam.

That's when she heard the first roar. It was a pleasant sound that echoed off the hills. But that didn't fool her; she was getting used to the reversals caused by the curse and knew that this roar, no matter how pleasant it sounded, was a grave thing.

Snatching back her hand, she stuffed the stone in her pocket and called, "Jassy."

"Laurel! Let's go."

And then, the second roar.

She crashed through the bushes toward Jassy's voice. She hadn't combed her hair or taken a drink or eaten, but that didn't matter.

When Laurel finally saw Jassy, she stopped short, suddenly overcome with shame and loneliness and worry. "The Hallvard?" she asked.

Jassy grabbed up her pack and threw it at her. "Yes, he's coming, but we'll make it." Turning, he grabbed up his pack and pulled out a hunk of bread. "Eat as you go.

The Hallvard is still a long way away, but we need to go now. The rain washed away our scent and tracks. I think if we get across the river quickly, we'll lose him. Just walk. Don't think about the Hallvard."

Laurel took the bread, nodded and followed Jassy down the trail.

But of course, she couldn't stop thinking about the Hallvard. His yellow eyes watching her. She crowded Jassy, urging him to go faster until they were trotting at an even pace.

Even the curse couldn't hide her weariness: Laurel ached all over, especially the heel of her left foot where a blister was rubbing. It irritated her that her damp, wrinkled clothes felt like silk, that her dirty hair felt glossy, that her travel bread tasted like spiced cake. They splashed through puddles, puddles that felt warm but should feel cold. She knew that it was all wrong, but even that didn't matter. Instead, there was only a fear that grew with each step.

Her heart throbbed, keeping time with her pounding steps. Pushing her: Go faster. Go! Go! Go!

....

TWENTY-ONE

G o! Go! Go! Laurel ran and as she ran, she remembered other times, other memories of when she had raced here or there: she remembered the priest's surprise when she toddled down the aisle of the cathedral, laughing at the colored lights from the windows and trying to catch that light in her hands; she looked back to laugh at her father as he chased her up the steps of the bell tower, or up and down the scaffolding for the east tower; she looked into the quarry and raced down the steep, steep path to leap into the quarry master's arms; she watched herself walk through the city gates, and then break into a run as she wondered if Jassy would be waiting for her, watching the path to see if she would come and visit the Rover cave. She didn't know why these images haunted her as she ran; she just ran and let them wash over and through her. And when the memories finally faded, she felt like a lifetime had passed. The memories left her exhausted. And she was surprised to find the sun high overhead, to find that half the day had passed. And she was still running.

*   *   *

"How far have we come?" Laurel panted. She leaned against a tree trunk and clutched the stitch in her side. Her pack lay at her feet.

"Not sure," Jassy said. He was trying to catch his breath, too. "Halfway through the woods? We still have to cross the river, and then it's half a day's walk up the hillside."

It irritated her that his linen shirt and grey britches looked spotless when she knew they were muddy. Even his spotless pack had to be soaked from running under wet branches. "I haven't heard anything behind us for a while."

Laurel's yellow skirt was likely splotched with red mud, too. Her blister had popped—no way the curse could change that feeling—and a new one was forming, but she had run on anyway.

Jassy blinked up at the sky. "So hot and muggy."

The clearing was ringed with yellow and pink flowering bushes which sent a cloying fragrance into the air that dragged at Laurel. She didn't ask if Jassy saw the flowers, smelled them. What was the point?

"Maybe we lost the Hallvard," Jassy said hopefully.

A deafening roar startled them.

"Oh! He's close." Laurel's heart pounded. She grabbed her jewel bag and backed away from the path.

With another roar, the Hallvard burst into the clearing. Laurel barely recognized the stone statue from the night before. The stern countenance had been transformed into an angelic smile, and he moved with ponderous, awkward steps. Mentally, she translated: a savage snarl and quick, graceful movements.

"Jassy! Do something!"

"What?"

The Hallvard stopped and rose on his hind legs. He shook his shaggy muzzle from side to side. He stopped. His nose pointed straight at Laurel.

Laurel jumped behind Jassy.

Jassy pushed her away. "What's going on?"

Laurel hid her bag behind her back. "It's mine."

The Hallvard dropped onto all fours and paced forward.

Laurel and Jassy retreated until her back hit the bushes at the edge of the clearing.

"You're a bear keeper. You should know what to do."

"It's not a bear; it's a Hallvard."

With prickly branches pressing against her back, Laurel watched the Hallvard draw closer and closer. Now, she could see even, white teeth—no. It didn't matter what she saw, it was wrong. She translated what she saw: The Hallvard had strong, yellow teeth and sickle-like claws.

"Jassy!"

"I know!" Jassy grabbed Laurel's bag and edged around the clearing away from her. The Hallvard stopped, as if uncertain which person to attack. Jassy's fingers tore at the knots on the bag.

"What are you doing?"

155

"Trying to save our lives," Jassy said grimly. He held up a clenched fist, full of pebbles, the fake jewels. The Hallvard half rose, following the motion of the jewels like a trained bear following his master's commands. It gave Laurel fresh hope. Maybe Jassy did know how to handle the Guardian.

Jassy flung the jewels over the Guardian's head.

The Hallvard twisted, trying to catch them with his paws. He roared in excitement—was that the reverse of frustration? —as the jewels disappeared into the undergrowth. He scrambled to where one landed and scratched in the leaves, searching for it.

Jassy caught up their packs and both jewel bags and raced to Laurel. He grabbed her hand and pulled. "Run! It'll take him a while to find the jewels."

Laurel jerked her jewel bag from Jassy and hugged it as they dashed from the clearing and down the trail.

Behind them, the Hallvard roared. In triumph, Laurel thought, trying to interpret what she heard.

"He's found one jewel," Jassy called over his shoulder. "Hurry! We've got to cross the creek before–"

"Coming." Laurel was breathing hard, but she knew they couldn't stop. The jewel in her skirt pocket burned into her leg, almost tripping her. She tried to ignore it. The Hallvard is only after our bags of jewels, she told herself. She knew Jassy had done the only thing he knew to do—buy time with a few jewels.

Laurel splashed through endless puddles and jumped over limbs that had broken off in the night's storm. Her legs grew heavier and weaker, but each time she slowed, they heard a bellow of triumph that told them the Hallvard had found another jewel.

After the fourth time, Laurel called to Jassy, "How many did you throw?"

He slowed and ran beside her. "Don't know," he said panting. "Maybe, one more."

Laurel tried to calculate how fast they were running and how fast the Hallvard could run. He was faster than they were, and he wouldn't tire as easily. Would they be far enough ahead to cross the creek before the Hallvard caught them?

Laurel and Jassy both held their sides, now. Their breathing was labored and rough. But they dared not stop.

Slowly, Laurel realized she was hearing something strange. It was a dull thrumming that grew steadily. It puzzled her, but she couldn't worry about it now. It took more and more concentration just to keep moving. By now, she was limping badly, her blister raw and aching, so that she could barely trot. She was mad and tired and hurting. And it's Jassy's fault, she thought.

Suddenly, she ran into Jassy, but he was ready for her and merely caught her in his circle of arms and made her stand still.

"Shhh! Listen. Have you heard the Hallvard lately?"

"What?"

Jassy waggled his pointy gargoyle ears and listened for any sound of pursuit. "He's got to be coming."

Jassy reached for the jewel bag that Laurel still clutched. She swiveled away and lashed out, trying to scratch Jassy's ugly face. "Don't touch my jewels."

Jassy dropped his hands and stared. "Have you lost your mind?"

Now, Laurel stopped to really look. She shivered in the cold wind and stared up at bare branches. Was it really winter? Why was she arguing with Jassy? He was the only steadfast thing in this crazy land. Two in, two out. He wouldn't try to leave without her.

Seeing her confusion, Jassy gently took the jewel bag, and then took her hand and pulled her along toward the noise in front of them.

They came out of the woods into the cold sunshine and stared at the dirty stream. The rivulets had fed the creeks; the creeks had tumbled toward larger streams; the streams had paraded madly to the river. The stream they had crossed the day before was now a river, a torrent of water cascading through boulders, barely staying within the banks.

Behind them, the Hallvard roared, louder and closer.

Beyond the tumult, Laurel saw the path rising up the hill. She caught a red gleam from the Troll's Eye doorway far above them. It might as well be a thousand leagues away. That hallucination she saw, that bridge, it wasn't there. There was no way to cross the river.

TWENTY-TWO

F aced with the river at flood stage, Jassy made an instant decision. "We'll go upstream and look for a place to ford."

Laurel waved him forward, and then hobbled along behind. Despite the illusion of a wide-open path, the riverbank was hard to follow. She kept bumping into trees which grew right down to the edge of the banks where many large oaks and willows hung out over the rushing water. They climbed over or went around huge tree trunks. The ground itself was hard-packed—no, it was spongy and so waterlogged that each step took effort, and progress was agonizingly slow.

The river wound around the base of the cliff. Each minute took them farther upstream, away from the trail up the cliff, until Laurel was ready to scream. They had a day and a half before they had to be out of this wretched land. But it rankled her to waste any time going upriver.

Laurel worried about the Hallvard gaining on them, but apparently, he couldn't travel fast off the path, either. Sometimes they heard him roar over the sound of rushing water, but they kept their lead.

Mid-afternoon, Jassy split half a loaf. "It's the last of the bread. I hope we'll be out by nightfall, but just in case, we need to save some for tomorrow."

Laurel was weary and grateful for anything; she broke off bits and chewed hard at the spice-cake-flavored brick as she plodded along. She tried to keep up with Jassy, but her feet grew heavier.

They'd gone perhaps two or three miles—at a snail's pace—when Jassy stopped and pointed. "Do you think we could jump those?"

Laurel didn't bother to look: "Describe it to me."

Jassy explained that the river had gradually narrowed until now two large boulders, which lay on each side of the river, were only five or six arm-spans apart. It was the narrowest spot they'd seen yet, but water shot through this narrow cataract with a violent roar.

Laurel was thin and short and always aware that she was the architect's daughter or sometimes a nurse for the town folk; she had a rich life with connections throughout her community. And now, her life came down to this, her ability to jump, to make a mighty leap across swift waters, deep inside this stone world, where she could be lost forever. It was a simple thing to ask, that leap. "No. I'll fall."

A growl rumbled through the woods behind her.

"You have no choice," Jassy said. "I'll jump first, and then catch you when you jump."

Laurel shivered. Then, she shrugged, "I don't care. Try it."

Jassy scampered up the rock. It was wide enough to allow three or four running steps. Grinning in such intense concentration, his dark brows looked like angel wings.

He needs wings to make it, Laurel thought.

Jassy took a deep breath, then ran and leaped. He arched out over the water and hung for a moment at the top, like a gargoyle bat. Then he came down and landed squarely on the rock on the opposite shore.

He leaped and shouted angrily, "Hurrah!"

Laurel dredged up enough energy to smile.

"Your turn! Come on!"

Laurel grasped the rock and climbed. The rock was covered with smooth gray-green lichens and emerald mosses. She stared at three tiny ferns that hung in a crevice above the water, trying to avoid looking at the smooth water below them. Were the ferns real? Was it really a torrent of water?

She backed away from the edge. Looking up, she shook her head.

Jassy stood at the edge of his rock and held out his hands: they were gargoyle hands, of course, with bone-thin fingers, hairy palms, grasping and groping hands made for stealing jewels.

"Come on!"

Laurel backed farther away and whispered, "No."

The Hallvard lumbered out of the woods, and when it saw Laurel, it roared. The sound—like an organ playing a hymn in the cathedral—reverberated off the blood-red cliffs above them. The beast charged straight for her rock.

It was now or never.

She closed her eyes for a moment. It didn't matter if Jassy was a gargoyle or not, she had to jump. She clung to the rope of the jewel bag. She opened her eyes, ran two quick steps and leapt.

Over the tiny ferns.

Stretching across the water.

Straining to reach the far rock.

Her fingers caught the edge of the boulder, the jewels banging against the rock. Then her hand slipped on the wet moss. Jassy grabbed her arm and held on, giving her some stability. Laurel pulled, straining arm muscles, while trying to find a foot hold. At last, she lay halfway on top, and Jassy gave one more heave, but as he did, she looked at his hands. Hallvard paws!

Startled, Laurel jerked away.

She fell.

Hot water hit Laurel with a shock and she sank deep, deeper, tumbling until a current caught her. She fought, kicking hard, and finally broke the surface to gulp in air. Then the rapids pulled her under again. Her hand was still wrapped around the cord of the jewel bag and it weighed her down. But she wouldn't let it go. She needed those jewels, she thought fiercely. She had a cathedral to build.

From deep inside, Laurel found a reserve of strength and kicked again. She broke the surface, gasping, coughing. This time, she was out of the main current and could stay afloat. She tried to get her bearings. The cliffs were to her right and she was on the left side of the current. Moaning, she realized it was the Hallvard's side of the river.

Laurel tried to windmill her arms, a crude swimming motion, trying to reach Jassy's side. Instead, the current swept her even further downstream. She was small and thin and weighed down by sodden skirts and a heavy bag of jewels. She couldn't swim across the river.

She turned and kicked back toward the wrong shore. The water became shallower until, eventually, Laurel's feet touched bottom and in a few more strokes, she stood upright.

"The Hallvard!" Jassy's voice was dim above the river's music.

Looking upstream, Laurel saw the Hallvard pushing through bushes toward her. She shoved wet hair from her face–she'd never had time to comb it out and braid it–and realized that she was trapped in the middle of the river.

"Jewels! Throw jewels!"

Jassy's advice was probably wise. Though they felt nimble, Laurel's fingers were obviously cold and stiff and the knot in the jewel bag was wet and stubborn. Just one jewel, she thought. Just one. Let Jassy waste his, but she needed all of hers.

Then, she started shivering with cold. She wrapped her arms around herself and tried to stop shaking. The only warm place on her body was the stone in her pocket, which burned on her thigh.

163

The Hallvard cleared the underbrush and loped toward her.

Desperate, she fumbled again with the knot.

The Hallvard closed in.

The knot came loose. Laurel pulled out one jewel and pitched it over the beast's head.

He didn't slow down or even blink his yellow eyes. With a mighty sweep of his paw, he uprooted a bush in his way. Now, he rose onto two legs, towering over Laurel as he had in the cave. He advanced, arms outstretched, and she could only imagine him flexing his massive claws.

Laurel jerked out a handful of stones and threw them over the Hallvard's head. He was close enough now for Laurel to hear him grunting.

He hesitated but came on anyway.

Now, Laurel threw handful after handful over his head, into the woods, into the river. The jewels arced like rainbows through the sky. Desperately, she threw a handful at his feet.

The Hallvard stopped and dropped onto all fours. He picked up a jewel, his paws surprisingly adept. He had a fur pouch of some sort strapped across his belly into which he deposited each jewel he found.

Laurel waded back into the river until it was waist high. She splashed upstream, hurrying past the now-occupied Hallvard and looking back often, expecting the beast to be at her heels. But he was busy now, finding the jewels. Laurel climbed back up the bank and ran to the boulders.

Chilled, almost unable to move for shivering, Laurel lay flat on her stomach, watching the Hallvard and letting the warmth from the stone seep in. Each time the beast put a stone in its pouch, she shook her head and fumed. Those were her jewels.

Before she was really ready, she forced herself to stand and face the gap between boulders again. Jassy was there, waiting for her. She took a deep breath, ran and jumped.

And landed beside Jassy, on her feet.

Jassy grabbed her and hugged, and then immediately pulled her away, back downstream to where they could pick up the trail again.

TWENTY-THREE

A t last Jassy and Laurel stood at the bottom of the cliff trail. Laurel tilted her head back, hoping for a glimpse of the Troll's Eye doorway, but it was hidden from view. She sat on a boulder and rubbed her right calf. "My legs ache."

Jassy studied the cliff, too. "We need to move faster. It took us half a day to hike down this hill and walking up will be even slower."

"When the sun goes down, the Hallvard is stone, right? We can rest then." Now, her fingers probed the ache in her left calf.

"No! That's when we need to climb."

She stretched her toes long, and then tilted them upward, but still her calves hurt. She used a long, firm stroke to rub the right calf again.

Jassy smiled, making his face look open and rested. "I don't understand. Why is the Hallvard chasing us anyway?"

"Why are you asking me?"

Jassy sank to his haunches and stared straight at her face. Their gazes locked. Jassy had a silly grin on his face that Laurel translated: he was scowling.

"Maybe we're being chased because Master Gimpel lied."

"Is there something you're not telling me?"

Laurel bent to retie her shoes. Did he suspect? She wanted to check the stone in her pocket but forced herself to take her time with each shoelace. Then she sat up and glared at Jassy. "You want all the jewels for yourself? Well, stay away from mine. Throw yours to the Hallvard, if you want, but I'm keeping the rest of mine."

Jassy grinned at her so hard that his eyebrows became one straight black line. He opened his mouth to say something, and then snapped it shut. He stood and started trotting up the trail.

Laurel watched him for a moment and then rose and followed. What else could she do? Two in, two out.

Silence reigned while they ascended the cliff, and the darkness crept across the sky. Laurel desperately wanted to reach up and force the sun below the horizon so the Hallvard would sleep. Her calves were aching again and threatening to cramp up. Instead, she plodded along, just like the sun plodded along.

The path was steeper than she had remembered. Looking back down the cliff, they were high enough now that she could no longer see separate trees, just the forest canopy. She looked up to where Jassy was, above her on the trail. A short way off the path, she caught a flash of white.

"Jassy, wait."

She walked toward the white and peered through the growing dusk. "It's a tiny canyon, look. There's something back here." She stopped at a cliff face that opened into a box-shaped area.

She stood before a mound of dirt. "Jassy, what is it?"

"Laurel, we don't have time." He was in the opening of the box canyon. Then, he came briskly toward her. "It's a grave." He put his hand on something at the end of the dirt mound. "This is a white cross." He hesitated, but then described it, telling her about the bleached white wood that was tied together into a crude cross, and a green vine with white flowers twined around it.

Laurel thought: There's something I should know about a vine and flower. But she couldn't think what.

Hoarse, Laurel whispered, "Who is buried here?"

"There's a name carved on the cross. Gimpel."

"His brother?" Laurel asked. "There's too much here we don't know."

Jassy nodded, and it was a tired nod, as if the simple act of moving his head up and down was impossible. And Laurel remembered that first time she saw him outside the cathedral, his face as he studied the cathedral and later, when he concentrated on collecting coins, the passion and energy of his smile, his patter. Was he really tired now, or full of energy? She hated not knowing. She plucked one of the flowers, still wondering why she was supposed to notice it. Touching the white wood, Laurel was surprised at how smooth it felt. "Jassy, promise—"

Jassy whirled and put a finger to her mouth to stop her from saying more. "Two in, two out," he whispered.

Laurel blinked, her eyes suddenly full of tears. "Jassy."

Suddenly, the canyon darkened even more, and they spun to see the Hallvard's massive body blocking the entrance. Laurel jumped up and searched the canyon walls for an exit. The walls were three times a man's height, smooth and sheer. There was only one entrance and exit, a perfect box.

Jassy grabbed her hand. "Only a few minutes till the sun sets."

But the Hallvard seemed to understand the urgency of his situation. He advanced quickly.

"Separate," Jassy said. "Confuse him."

Laurel darted right, while Jassy went left. The beast followed Laurel and in two quick steps, trapped her in a corner. She had no weapons, nothing to use for defense. Instinct took over. She grabbed the ties of her jewel bag and whipped it around like a slingshot. Just as it came around, the Hallvard slashed out, his claws ripping out the bottom. Jewels—the worthless pebbles—flew in all directions, some landing on the canyon floor, some on the grave. And before Laurel could do anything, the Hallvard lashed out again. She ducked. But his claws caught her face. She fell, clutching wildly at her face, at her eye. She almost swooned at the pain, even as she rolled away, expecting to be crushed.

Nothing.

Laurel rolled back over, unable to rise because of pain, barely able to look up. The Hallvard was frozen, his feet hard rock and as she watched, the transformation traveled up his body. His eyes hardened into brilliant yellow jewels that glittered with malice.

The sun had set.

TWENTY-FOUR

J assy pulled Laurel away from the stone Hallvard. She was faint with pain, so he pulled her arm over his shoulder and they staggered out of the box canyon. At the trail, he eased her down to lean against the cliff. Jassy tore open his pack, searching for something to staunch the flow of blood. He grabbed his spare shirt and a knife and hacked the shirt into several pieces and put one piece in Laurel's hand. She pressed it to her face, moaning.

Jassy quickly found wood, started a fire with his flint, filled the small pot with water from his water skin and put it on to boil. Laurel was shivering now in the hot evening air. Jassy rolled a stone near the fire and helped her move to lean against it where the fire could keep her warm.

Now, Jassy lit a stick from the fire and held it high. He motioned for Laurel to remove the cloth. Laurel watched his face as she took it off: his eyes lit up and he grinned.

"That bad?" she demanded, and then regretted it. Speaking made her very aware of the injury: she could feel that the Hallvard's claws had caught her forehead, eyebrow, the corner of her right eye—which was already swollen shut, and her cheek.

Jassy dipped another cloth into the frigid water and squeezed it out, leaving it just damp. He turned back to her and murmured. "You'll have scars. And this will hurt."

At his touch, Laurel cried out and thrust him away.

"You have to let me clean it," he said, his voice cold and harsh.

With her good eye, she saw that his cheek was twitching, and she guessed that he was having a hard time keeping control of his emotions. There was something she should remember, though. What?

Then, she knew. It hurt to speak, her jaw movements like stabs. "On the cross. Vine. White star flowers."

"You think it's the flower the Master Gimpel mentioned?"

Laurel barely nodded, and then closed her good eye. She heard Jassy run back into the canyon. Suddenly, she panicked, "Jassy!" Oh, the pain! She rocked back and forth, not caring if he heard her or not.

"I'm here." Jassy knelt beside her and put her hand on a rough flower. "What do I do with them?"

She peeked at the flower: could petals that rough and thin be worth anything? Still, they had no other herbs to try. Speaking from one side of her mouth, she whispered. "Infusion. Boil them. Then bathe my face."

And while Jassy made great echoing sounds around the fire and pot, Laurel concentrated, trying to ease her pain: she thought about how much she hated the bald clerics who controlled the hated purse that controlled building of the cathedral; how much she hated the Gargoyle Man who had tricked her into looking through the hated Troll's Eye; how she hated the Hallvard who only wanted the jewel in her pocket. She fingered the white flower that still lay in her hand, and then crammed it into her mouth and chewed slowly, letting the sweet apple-like flavor fill her mouth, concentrating on keeping her mouth marching in time to the throb of her cheek. She would fool them all. She would never give up.

*　　*　　*

Laurel woke to the smell of rotten fruit. She smiled to herself; Father had forgotten again to take the supper tray back down to Symon. But the smile shot pain through her face. She reached up, tentative, exploring and felt rough bandages around her head. She remembered: the Hallvard had clawed her.

But why were they still here, sleeping, when they should be trying to get home before dawn when the Hallvard woke again?

Laurel pushed herself upright. Every muscle hurt: her hip was bruised from the fall into the river, and her face throbbed. Only one thing felt good. Her hand crept into her pocket and found the jewel. It was safe.

Across the fire, Jassy's head lolled on his pack. Around his head and neck, he wore garlands of some plant, probably the green vine with the white star flowers. Laurel stood and had to hang with her head down for a minute for a dizzy spell to pass. Then she limped around the fire and shook Jassy's shoulder.

He woke with a start. "How long did I sleep? Are you all right?"

"We must run," she mumbled. With no stars or moon, it was black in this stone world, except for the red embers of the fire, impossible to tell the time.

Jassy rubbed his eyes, and then poked at the coals and added more wood until the light flared up. Then he dished up a crude stew he had made with jerky. "Eat. You need strength for the climb."

Despite the putrid smell, Laurel ate greedily at first. Her jaw movement still made her face hurt, though it didn't throb like before. Still, she stopped eating before the bowl was half empty. Jassy finished her bowl and another besides. Then he rapidly washed the pot and bowls and repacked them. Now there was only the pot with the flower infusion left to deal with.

"Let's change the dressing on your face."

Laurel didn't like it, but knew it needed to be done.

Jassy unwrapped the cloths and held up the torch. With a puzzled look, he said, "Better already."

"Will it scar?"

"Maybe not. The flowers are working better than I expected."

"A miracle?"

"A miracle," he agreed. He replaced the dressing with fresh cloths soaked in the flower infusion. Then he soaked the rest of his cloths in the infusion, dumped out the remainder, and put the cloths back into the pot to keep them damp. Finally, his pack was ready.

"Let's go." He offered his gargoyle hand to Laurel. But she lifted one of the vines that still hung around his neck. "Put these in your pack, too."

While he did that, she said, "Jassy, I've been thinking. The Hallvard is just rock now, right? Why don't we try to break that rock apart? Push him over, drop a boulder on him, and push him off a cliff. Something. Anything."

"While he can't strike back." Jassy pulled her to her feet. "It might work."

Carrying the torch, they went back to the box canyon. Laurel followed slowly and wondered how she would be able to make it up the cliff path if this didn't work. The blister on her heel was better but still chafed, her hip hurt, her face ached, and she could only see from one eye. At the canyon's opening, she leaned against the stone and watched Jassy.

The torchlight threw a tiny Hallvard shadow against the opposite wall, making him look like a wooly lamb. Laurel shivered. How long till dawn and he woke again? If only they knew.

Jassy motioned her forward to hold the torch. He put his shoulder behind the Hallvard's knee and shoved. The massive form didn't budge.

"Too heavy," Jassy said, panting.

Laurel held the torch high and looked upward. "Maybe there are rocks to push over on top of him."

"Let's look. But we must be quick."

They turned to leave the box canyon, but Laurel stopped, puzzled. "Where are the jewels?" She remembered now that the Hallvard had ripped open her bag and scattered the jewels.

"I picked them up," Jassy said. "When we get out, we'll split them."

Laurel didn't answer, not wanting the pain of talking again. But she was pleased. Jassy's jewels didn't matter except as a way to slow down the Hallvard. They had two real treasures to take back: her Troll's Eye and the flowers to heal Antonio and Father. Two treasures and two miracles. A new cathedral and Father healed and ready to direct the construction. Then she could stay on, too, and learn to carve. She wouldn't have to marry, wouldn't have to leave. It was worth even a small scar on her face.

They scrambled up the slope outside the canyon. Jassy pointed out a boulder that was a rich red like the cathedral wall and was twice his arm span. "Looks like it's in the right position and big enough."

Laurel held the torch again so Jassy could shove the boulder. It rocked but didn't roll.

"You'll have to help," Jassy said.

They propped the torch against another boulder. Laurel grabbed a stick—she hoped it was a sturdy one but couldn't really tell—and waited until Jassy heaved again. When the boulder rocked, she shoved the stick under it. He heaved again, and Laurel wedged the stick farther under the boulder. Jassy shoved and Laurel levered with the stick, afraid it would break. But the boulder started to roll. Laurel grabbed the torch and they watched. The boulder tumbled, bouncing once, twice, off the cliff before it hit the Hallvard full in the face. An explosion boomed, echoing throughout the valley. Rock dust floated up toward Jassy and Laurel, blocking their vision for a moment.

When it cleared, Laurel grabbed Jassy's arm. "Look."

The boulder had shattered into thousands of tiny pieces, while the Hallvard stood upright and unharmed. "We can't destroy him," Laurel said.

"But he can destroy us."

The boulder was now shattered rock, like her hopes were shattered. She wanted to scoop up the pieces and glue them back together, but there was only one thing that mattered now.

"Run." She said it softly, but the word echoed.

And from below, the Hallvard growled softly in return, almost an echo.

"Run, Jassy, run."

They ran. They scurried down the slope to their camp and grabbed the pack and jewel bags. A brisk wind blew down the valley and along the creek and the path. Torchlight jerked as they ran, shadows startling her and adding to her growing panic. *Run, Jassy, run*, she thought.

They made progress. Not fast, but enough that Laurel's panic started to ebb away and hope return. Then Jassy stopped: "Look."

The eastern sky was grey with a crimson stain that spread across the horizon.

"Curses! Why did we sleep so long? Faster, Laurel."

She tried to obey, but with the coming of dawn, the curse overwhelmed her, and she trotted in a dreary winter world, cold and miserable. There were no squirrels, no birds, no river music. Instead, the rocky path was full of rubble and debris, making it an impossible path to follow even if she had been uninjured.

They climbed in spurts now, alternately running, and then plodding, for an hour before the sun rose fully and Jassy called that he saw the Hallvard's black form silhouetted against the red rocks of the cliff. The Guardian of the treasure cave was toiling up the slope behind them. They were only a quarter of the way up the hillside, and their pace was too slow. But Laurel could go no faster.

It was another few hours before the Hallvard was close enough that Jassy stopped to decoy him by throwing a couple jewels over the beast's head. The jewels bounced off the cliff and into the crevasses below. The Hallvard raged, but to Laurel, his roar sounded like an accomplished opera singer. Obviously, he was angry. But he backtracked to find the jewels.

Laurel trotted now with one hand in her pocket, cradling her treasure. She moved automatically, as if sleepwalking. "Two in, two out. Two treasures, two miracles." She chanted the words and moved her feet.

Jassy half-carried her over rough areas, and they pulled ahead of the Hallvard again. But through the haze of pain and self-hypnosis, Laurel could feel herself tiring. She needed to rest. Sleep. Just two minutes.

No. Two in, two out. Two treasures, two miracles. She caressed her stone and moved her feet.

By mid-afternoon, they were about halfway up the cliff when Laurel sagged without warning onto a flat rock and curled up to sleep.

"Laurel, run."

"Two minutes," she murmured. Then she slept.

*   *   *

Jassy shook Laurel, and she sat up instantly.

I couldn't have slept even five minutes, she thought. But it seemed as if a huge boulder had been lifted off her chest. She yawned and carefully stretched sore muscles. Then she saw Jassy: his face was lit up, his face so brilliant that she hardly knew him. Oh, she thought, he must be furious about something.

"What's this?" Her Troll's Eye twinkled in his hand.

Laurel blinked her good eye, and then groped in her pocket. Empty. "That's mine!"

"You took an extra jewel!" he accused flatly. "I was looking for a clean piece of cloth to bathe your cuts. And I found this."

"In the cave, everything looked like river pebbles except this one. I'm sure it's another Troll's Eye."

"Don't you understand what you've done?" Jassy exploded. "You couldn't be content with two full bags? You had to have just one more?"

"It's just one." Laurel was puzzled by his anger.

Below, the Hallvard sang in triumph.

Jassy pointed to the beast lumbering up the path toward them. "That's the difference. He won't stop until he gets this jewel. I'm going to give it to him." He hefted the red jewel and raised his arm to throw.

Laurel heaved herself up at Jassy and knocked his arm. The jewel dropped with a thunk and rolled toward the edge of the cliff. Laurel dove after it, grabbing it before it fell over.

"It's mine. Do you hear me? Mine!"

She stood before Jassy in a rage. In a strange way, she knew what she looked like: her hair was matted and stringy, her face was swathed in bandages, her clothes were filthy, and her fist was clenched around the Troll's Eye. She looked more like a gargoyle than a girl. And holding the Eye again, she felt the heaviness return. But she couldn't give it up; she had carried it so long. She was, well, fond of the jewel. Some part of her knew that "fond" was the wrong word, but she hadn't the strength to figure out what word she should use. Probably "obsessed."

"We'll never make it," Jassy said. His voice was emotionless, his features clear. He sat on the flat rock and crossed his legs. "We'll wait here for the Hallvard."

"So now you want to give up? Well, I won't let you. I need you: two in, two out." Laurel jerked open the jewel bag. She shook out a handful of the worthless pebbles and flung them over the Guardian's head.

The beast turned doggedly to recover them.

"See? We'll make it. Only two more hours," Laurel cried. "And if we only bring out this one Troll's Eye, it will be worth it."

She slung her back pack over her shoulders and hobbled determinedly up the path.

Jassy yelled after her, "You're a fool, Laurel!" It echoed and re-echoed off the blood-red cliffs: "Fool–Laurel–fool."

....

TWENTY-FIVE

Laurel and Jassy trudged uphill, now and then jogging a step or two, but too tired to do more than that.

In some odd way, this trek up the hillside was a happy time for Laurel, maybe the happiest of her life. First, she was working for something important, trying harder than ever before, striving, straining. It wasn't easy, like kneeling to pray was easy. Nor was it easy like tending the sick was easy when you had the right herbs and knew what to do with them. Nothing was easy here because it was hard, unknown. It was hard because everything was reversed. But part of the joy came in that difficulty. No one else was doing this thing because it was too scary, too hard. But Laurel had taken the risk, had been willing to suffer for something bigger than herself, for the cathedral and her father's health and her own future. She was happy because this struggle was for all the right reasons.

Of course, the knowledge that she carried a Troll's Eye was a happy thing, too. She kept her hand in her pocket, rubbing her thumb against the stone's cut surface. If only Jassy appreciated the jewel, it would truly be a happy moment, to share that with him.

Barely noticing the trail, Laurel walked onward, climbing towards the way out of this stone world.

And now the red glow of the Troll's Eye door was guiding them. They were close, maybe thirty minutes away. But the sun was low and the Hallvard was closing in.

*   *   *

Jassy shook out the jewel bag. Empty. He threw it over the cliff in frustration. "He's coming fast!"

Laurel was exhausted. They charged up the last slope—if their agonizing pace could be called charging–to the plateau with the Troll's Eye door. They sped through the corridor formed by the linden trees. At the corridor's end, through the hazy light of the Troll's Eye, the Gargoyle Man appeared as a giant.

"Master Gimpel, we're back!" Jassy yelled.

The mason didn't look up from the stone on which he was working.

With her good eye, Laurel saw the Hallvard climb up onto the plateau on the outside of the linden tree corridor. Apparently, he had abandoned the path and climbed straight up the cliff. She grabbed Jassy's arm and pointed.

"Run!" Jassy cried.

They sprinted, forcing fatigued muscles to move beyond their limit. The Hallvard dropped to all fours and raced with astonishing speed. But Laurel and Jassy had a head start.

Laurel called, triumphant, "We'll make it!"

Then, she caught her foot on a rock, stumbled, fell. She was up in an instant, but now the Hallvard had the edge. He reached the Troll's Eye door first. He rose onto his hind legs to block the exit.

Jassy called, "Laurel, do you smell that? It's the herbs you spread on the workshop floor."

Almost home!

The Hallvard roared, almost like a guffaw. The note of joy in the bellow paralyzed Laurel. The Hallvard took a step toward her.

Jassy jumped in front of Laurel, shoving her backward and held both arms out as a shield. His voice melodic, he ordered her, "Give him the jewel."

"No." She clamped her jaw and searched for something to distract the beast.

"Laurel, now! We'll be trapped here."

"No!" There had to be another way.

"Look! The doorway is shrinking! We have no time!"

But Laurel couldn't give up now. She had scars on her face, and she had to have something to show for that. Around them, the darkness was gathering, leaving the Hallvard illuminated solely by the red light of the Troll's Eye. As the sun set, though, the doorway was starting to close.

"Stall him until his feet turn to stone."

"That'll be too late!"

"No! It's mine!" She held the Troll's Eye in her clenched fist and shook it fiercely at the boy and the beast. "Mine."

Jassy grabbed Laurel's fist. She struggled, but Jassy was stronger. He wrenched the stone away and wheeled around to the Hallvard. It lunged at them, but Jassy threw the stone aside. He ducked under the beast's arm, seized Laurel's hand and pulled her to the Eye. Just as the ball of sun was disappearing beneath the horizon, so too, the doorway home was disappearing.

Laurel strained against Jassy's pull, back toward the jewel. She had to get it before the Hallvard. But the beast already had it, was holding it up. The last rays of the sun caught the Troll's Eye, and red flashes of light darted across the plateau.

And the Hallvard's feet started turning to granite.

"He's turning to stone, let me get my jewel!" Laurel twisted her hand away.

"No time! Two in, two out! It's now or never!"

Jassy stepped through the Troll's Eye and yanked Laurel with him. They were almost home.

Laurel watched him disappear, saw her own hand approach the red of the door. But that hand felt weightless, felt empty, felt wrong. It needed—demanded—the heavy weight of a Troll's Eye.

She jerked away, letting Jassy fall into the workshop, while she whirled around, raced to the Hallvard and plucked the Troll's Eye from his frozen, stone claws. Her thumb made tiny circles around the smooth surface of the jewel, and she smiled. She turned and darted for the doorway.

The red, glass-like door was now the size of a window. She ran full tilt and intended to leap through head first, but she banged into something as solid as a rock. Laurel shook her head and pushed at the window with her hands. She couldn't get through it.

She saw Jassy: he was rolling on the floor of the workshop, holding his head and moaning, every sound in the workshop now echoing in the stone world, too. In panic, Laurel pounded her fist against the red glass. But the doorway was solid–and shrinking.

Laurel snatched up a rock and smashed against the red glass, but it didn't even scratch its surface.

The Gargoyle Man came up to the Eye and bent to look through the jewel. All she saw was his eye.

And still the doorway dwindled.

The Gargoyle Man pulled back a bit, so she could see his face. He smiled. "Ah, now I know what to carve from this stone."

Laurel knelt before the tiny, tiny red window and pleaded, "Jassy! You promised. Don't leave me alone!"

She stuffed the jewel into her pocket and grabbed the opening with both hands, straining against the stone, trying to force it open.

The Gargoyle Man just smiled and said, "Good-bye."

And the Eye shrank.

And shrank.

Until it was just the size of an eye, the size of the original Troll's Eye jewel.

From her pocket, Laurel pulled out her own jewel and hefted it in her hand. Even knowing the cost, it burned in her hand and her mouth curved up with pleasure at its shape, its look, its feel against her skin.

Suddenly, from one of the linden trees came a familiar chirping. The red gargoyle bird flitted to a tree closer to her. From there, he tilted his impossibly long neck and looked at her quizzically.

"Oh," Laurel breathed. "You stayed with me. Come, sit on my shoulder." Jassy had left her, but the gargoyle bird had stayed. She wasn't alone.

But the bird just chirped again and waited.

She couldn't throw away her jewel. She couldn't. The bird flapped its wings and flew away from her. Just a few trees further, but he flew away.

Laurel knew what he wanted: she had to choose.

He was there to protect her, and he had stayed with her even if Jassy hadn't. It was the staying that mattered, not what you said. Yes, Jassy had tried to pull her with him, he had gone with her and supported her and tried to make her see that everything she did was because of the curse. She forgave him; it wasn't his fault that he went through the doorway without her.

But he wasn't here now. Only the gargoyle bird had truly stayed with her.

"Thank you," she whispered.

But the bird chirped and flapped away. Away to another tree further along the linden tree corridor.

Watching him, it was easier to raise her arm. Oh, they were heavy, reluctant to obey her, but she forced them to lift, while she kept her eyes on the gargoyle bird and listened to his chirping. She forced her hands to hurl the jewel away. It fell just short of the Hallvard, and he growled softly.

Suddenly, a great weight lifted. She was free of the curse of the Troll's Eye.

Just in time!

The night wind whistled up the valley, and she felt herself changing. Her feet were heavy, as heavy as marble. Then, the gargoyle bird was circling around her, soaring around her and singing the most beautiful song she had ever heard, and she closed her eyes and flew with him and sang with him until he decided to land on her shoulder.

Ah, she was not alone.

A sob caught in her throat, but Laurel refused to cry. She wouldn't give the Gargoyle Man a soul in agony to carve. Instead, she forced the weary muscles of her mouth to curve upward in a tranquil smile, the smile of a soul finally at peace.

The Troll's Eye doorway gave a final wink. Nightfall came to the stone world.

And Laurel was trapped forever in the blood-red stone.

TWENTY-SIX

....

63 Years Later

The spires of the Cathedral of St. Stephen were ablaze in color, a fiery stone prayer lighting up the morning sky. Snow fell in thick clumps from the thatched roofs. A soft warm wind brought the promise of an early spring. As morning broke, a Rover wagon jerked to a stop in front of the cathedral. A small girl with shiny black curls tumbled out, laughing and skipping in the bright sunshine. Her laughter was carried on the wind up to the highest point of the cathedral towers.

Laurel roused herself to listen and to watch.

An old man followed the child. "Wait for me, Bridgette."

"Grandfather Jassy, why do we stop here each spring?"

"To see an old friend."

"The gargoyle girl. Tell me the story again."

Jassy sat on a bench, and Bridgette sat beside him. Jassy was old now, his beard flowing white. He cleared his throat and began his story.

Jassy's familiar voice floated up to Laurel. He came each year to visit her, and for the last six years he'd brought little Bridgette and told her the story of their trip through the Troll's Eye.

"Don't forget to tell her about the two miracles!" whispered Laurel. *The wind caught her words and blew them toward the bench.*

Jassy cocked his head to the side for a moment, as if listening to the wind whisper to him. "Laurel was trapped in the stone. We couldn't do anything to make the Troll's Eye open again."

Bridgette climbed into his lap and ran soft fingers over his face and eye patch. "And your face was scarred when you went through the Troll's Eye alone."

"Yes, I am as ugly as that first Gargoyle Man."

She kissed his cheek. "I don't mind that you're ugly. I love you, anyway."

"The miracles! Tell her about the miracles!"

"But that's not all the story," Jassy continued. "Laurel was lost. We dared not tell Master Raymond where she really was. He thought she had been in the cave with Ana-Maria and Antonio and got lost on the way home. He thought wild beasts had attacked her in the forest, or someone carried her off. But one of the clerics remembered seeing her in the sanctuary.

"To honor her memory, they set her carving of the Christ child into a niche of the cathedral, along with a special offering box. All the money collected would go toward building the west tower. As word spread of the lost girl and her love of the cathedral, money began to come in from all over the country. Within the year, there was enough to start building the west tower. It was a miracle!" Jassy stood and took the little girl's hand. They walked closer to the cathedral.

"So, the west tower and turrets were built," Bridgette said with satisfaction. "Tell the rest."

"There was a second miracle. Master Raymond lived to see the whole of the west tower built. The star flowers healed him."

"And Antonio, too." Bridgette had heard the story so many times she knew what came next.

"Grandfather, where is Laurel now?"

Jassy stopped before the tower and looked up at the blood-red gargoyle on top of the turret. The tiny girl was shapely and comely, except for bulging eyes. One eye looked outward; the other was twisted and looked sideways. On her shoulder was a strange stone bird and on her face was a peaceful smile.

"The Gargoyle Man carved what he saw in the blood-red stone. He gave her eyes of stone to see our world. There she stands and will stand as long as the cathedral lasts. Multitudes will pass through the doors beneath her and never look up. They will never see her, but she sees them. She will see the generations come and go. And I don't know if she weeps or laughs."

The child smiled up at the gargoyle girl. "I think she's laughing at us right now. She got two miracles from the Troll's Eye."

"Are you happy, Laurel?" Jassy whispered. His wrinkled and scarred face was wet with tears.

"Two miracles," Laurel whispered to him. "It's all I asked for."

"Are you happy?" he repeated.

"I'm home," Laurel said. "The cathedral has always been my home."

Jassy knelt beside Bridgette and took her face in his large gentle hands. "Do you understand? The Troll's Eye was evil. You must never look through a Troll's Eye."

"Isn't the jewel gone forever?"

"It's gone," Jassy repeated. Then he adjusted his eye patch. "But after I die--if you find a Troll's Eye–you must promise to never look through a Troll's Eye."

"I promise," Bridgette said solemnly. Her black eyes stared quietly at the gargoyle girl.

Grandfather and granddaughter walked all around the cathedral, looking at the fantastic sculptures, at what some pilgrims called "the most spectacular gargoyles ever carved." And then they went inside to light a candle and pray for Laurel. An hour later, they came out.

Laurel watched them climb back into the Rover wagon. Jassy clucked to his white horses and drove off–north for the summer.

Laurel counted the years by his visits, sixty-three, so far. He wouldn't live very many more years. Laurel wondered if the granddaughter would come to visit her. Bridgette was so much like Jassy, so curious. She would find the Troll's Eye when Jassy died. When the old Gargoyle Man died, Jassy had hidden the stone behind his own eye patch. The stone was too fascinating to throw away. While he lived, he could keep it hidden, but he wouldn't live forever. Jassy was a fool to take the chance. A fool!

Would Bridgette look through the Troll's Eye, or not?

Laurel tried to call after them. "Beware the Troll's Eye."

But they were long gone. Instead, the spring wind picked up her call and carried it in and out and over and around the cathedral spires until all the other gargoyles roused themselves and took up the cry: "Beware!"

ABOUT THE AUTHOR

Award winning author **DARCY PATTISON** writes about fantasy worlds, the possibilities that lie in the unknown, and the incredible power of the human spirit to endure and overcome.

OTHER FANTASY NOVELS
Vagabonds
Liberty

SCIENCE FICTION SERIES
The Blue Planets World Series
Envoys, Prequel (short story)
Sleepers, Book 1
Sirens, Book 2
Pilgrims, Book 3

OTHER CONTEMPORARY NOVELS
Longing for Normal
Road Whiz
Saucy and Bubba

For more, see MimsHouse.com/newsletter

CPSIA information can be obtained
at www.ICGtesting.com
Printed in the USA
LVOW12*1018220418
574431LV00007B/39/P